Playing for

Keeps

Happy reading

Michele Shriver

Michele Shriver

SMC Publishing

Playing for Keeps
By Michele Shriver
Copyright 2015 Michele Shriver
Published by SMC Publishing
All Rights Reserved

ISBN-13:

978-1508679882

ISBN-10:

1508679886

"Hockey seems completely lawless and, therefore, inexplicably sexy." - Rachel Nichols

CHAPTER ONE

Traded.

Colton Tremblay woke with a throbbing headache, an unfamiliar woman in his bed, and a phone call from his agent giving him the news that no hockey player wanted to hear a few days before training camp. He'd been traded to another team, and not just any other team. An expansion team. In San Antonio, Texas, of all places. "You can't be serious," he protested. "Please tell me this is an April Fool's joke or something." In September, not likely. Maybe Scotty's idea of a really bad prank?

"No joke, Colton," Scotty Barlow said. "The trade call with the league is complete. As of fifteen minutes ago, you're officially the new center for the San Antonio Generals. Congratulations."

Colton grimaced. "You make it sound like this is a good thing."

"It could be a good thing," his agent said. "Look at it as a chance to remake your career. Fix your reputation."

"My reputation is fine. I won a Stanley Cup and the Conn Smythe." He was the hometown hero, the local boy, drafted first overall by the Montreal Canadiens and leading them back to Cup glory in only his second season. Now they were ready to cast him aside, shipping him off to an expansion team? Thanks for nothing, Montreal.

"That was three years ago," Scotty reminded him. "You could do no wrong then. Now everyone thinks stardom went to your head. You've lost focus. You party too much. You screw too many women. And the team missed the playoffs."

"Because our starting goalie missed fifty games with a back injury." Were they seriously trying to blame the team's collapse on Colton? "I scored ninety points. Only Crosby and Seguin had more." Third in the league in scoring, and they were cutting him loose. Clearly, someone in the organization decided Montreal wasn't big enough for both Colton and Brady McLean.

"Yeah, think about Seguin," Scotty said. "That trade to Texas worked out okay for him, huh?"

It had. No one could argue that. It wasn't the same, though. "That's different. Dallas already had a tradition of winning. San Antonio has… nothing. It's a fucking expansion team."

"Where you'll be the new face of the franchise. You can start over, be a leader on the team. Be an ambassador for the sport in a non-traditional market. You know the commissioner loves hockey in the south. I really think this is a great opportunity for you, Colton."

There seemed to be an unspoken 'So don't screw it up' implied at the end of his agent's statement. "If you say so," Colton said with a sigh. "Okay, give me the details."

He listened as his agent outlined the specifics of

the trade and told Colton he was expected to report to San Antonio by the following afternoon. Training camp would start the day after. "There's a conference call with the local media set up on Skype this afternoon," Scotty finished.

Colton exhaled. "Not wasting any time, huh?"

"No. The team's very excited to have you. They can't wait to get started," Scotty said. "You might want to learn some Spanish. Oh, and Colton?"

"What?"

"Get the woman out of your bed."

***

Maya Dominquez walked into San Antonio bureau of All Sports Today to find the office in chaos. Obviously breaking news of some sort. "What's going on?" she asked the news director.

"What's going on?" Frank Renner repeated. "Haven't you heard? The Generals just made a trade for Colton Tremblay. Colton Freaking Tremblay. Can you believe it?" Frank shook his head, as if the news was still sinking in. "I know the owner and the GM said they were serious about building a winning team right away, but I don't think anyone expected this."

Generals. Colton Tremblay. Maya tried to process it all as fast as possible. Hockey wasn't her number one sport, but she hadn't been living under a rock, either. Everyone in town was excited about San Antonio's new NHL franchise. As for the player Frank mentioned, Maya had no idea who he was. Judging from her boss's reaction, though, he must be a pretty big star. It wouldn't do to admit she'd never heard of the guy. If Maya ever wanted to move up from covering high school sports all over town to having her own beat, she needed to be an expert on all sports. "Wow," Maya said. "That should give the team immediate credibility."

"It sure will," Frank said. "As if the people in this town needed one more reason to be excited about finally getting an NHL team."

"It gives us plenty to report on too," Maya said. Whoever in the bureau who managed to score the new Generals beat would be plenty busy. Did Maya dare hope it might be her?

"Exactly." Frank ran a hand through his salt and pepper hair. "I've got a problem, though. Brad Smith called in sick, and the Generals have a video conference set up with Tremblay and the local media this afternoon. We have to be there." He looked at Maya. "Do you think you're ready for it, Dominguez?"

Was she ready for what? It took a few seconds for Frank's words to sink in. "You want me to cover the Generals press conference?" Maya couldn't quite believe it. It was what she wanted when she took the job with All Sports the year before, but she didn't know when—or if—she'd get the chance. Now Frank wanted her to cover the breaking news of the city's brand new NHL franchise.

"Yes. I'm in a bind here. We're shorthanded today, and you're a good reporter. I know this is a huge step up from what you've been doing, but I think you can handle it," Frank said. "Go show me what you're made of. Who knows. If you nail this assignment, you might just find yourself assigned as the regular beat reporter for the Generals."

A regular beat reporter? Maya tried not to get too carried away. It hadn't happened yet. "Thanks, Frank. I won't let you down."

He nodded. "I'm sure you won't. The call's at one. You better get ready."

One o'clock. Maya had a little less than four hours to learn everything she could about Colton Tremblay. He might be responsible for Maya getting her dream job.

***

The woman's name was Arianne, and she left her phone number on her way out the door, but Colton ripped it up and threw it in the trash. He wasn't much for repeat engagements and besides, in less than twenty-four hours, he'd be on a plane to Texas. For a born and bred Quebecian, it was a scary prospect. Colton would make it work, though. He had to. He didn't want to be one of those guys whose careers flamed out too early.

By the time the news conference rolled around, Colton was prepared. He had Scotty's best talking points rehearsed and he'd done a little research on his own. He even wore a brand new ball cap in the maroon and silver colors of his new team, and sporting the team's logo. How the hell Scotty managed to pull that off, Colton didn't know. He just knew the package had arrived by courier service and if he didn't wear it, he might be searching for a new agent.

Colton's phone rang a few minutes before one, and it was his new head coach. Paul Moreau was familiar to Colton, having coached Team Canada in the last Olympics, and if there was anything to look forward to about this move, it was the chance to play for a coach he respected.

"Colton, nice to talk to you again. Are you ready to come to San Antonio?"

"My flight's already booked, coach," he said. "I'll be there tomorrow. Looking forward to training camp and getting to know the rest of the guys."

"Perfect. I'll see you then. In the meantime, let's get this started." They went over the logistics of the

9

conference call, and the rules were pretty straightforward. Each of the news outlets that were present would get the opportunity to ask a question. After that, Colton could keep it going longer if he wanted to and allow some reporters to ask an additional question. Scotty had warned Colton that might be a dangerous practice, as reporters had egos and Colton didn't want to be seen as picking favorites. Don't play favorites, but be nice and accommodating to the press. Nothing like getting conflicting advice.

He called on the reporters in the front row first, fielding a variety of questions. How it felt to be traded. It sucked, but Colton didn't say that. How he expected hockey to be different in San Antonio than Montreal. He had no clue how to really answer that since he'd never been there. Hockey was hockey, he said. Every team environment was different and unique, but the sport was the same.

Colton moved to the second row. The reporter in the middle was a woman, and a gorgeous one at that, with silken black hair cascading to her shoulders. Okay, he'd always heard there were lots of beautiful women in Texas. If this one was any indication, the stories were true. Was she going to be covering the team? In that case, press conferences might not be so bad after all.

"Maya Dominguez from All Sports Today," she said, introducing herself. "How do you respond to reports that your fondness for women and night clubs led to this trade? Do you view this as an opportunity to salvage your image?"

So much for thinking maybe the female reporter would give him an easy question. No. Maya Dominguez might be a looker, but she'd done her homework too. She knew the stories out of Montreal. Fine. It was just as well that she asked about it. The sooner Colton could bury those reports and start fresh, the better.

"I don't read all the press, so I'm not familiar with everything that's been reported," Colton said, "but I think I got the gist of it. I don't like it, but I can't change what's been written. My play on the ice should speak for itself. I plan for it continue to do so. I'm coming to San Antonio to play hockey, first and foremost. My number one priority is trying to build the Generals into a winning team, not checking out the local nightclubs." Though he certainly wouldn't be opposed to that if the lovely Miss Dominguez wanted to accompany him. *Don't go there, Colton.* She may be hot, but she was a reporter. Forbidden fruit. "I do hope to have time to sample some great Mexican food, though," he added, flashing a smile.

***

"Great job, Dominguez," Frank praised when Maya got back to the bureau after the Generals press conference. "You did the prep work. You didn't play softball with the question. And it may have resulted in the best sound bite of the press conference."

Maya smiled at the compliment. "Thanks, Frank. And thanks for the opportunity." At least all of her research on the city's new hockey star paid off.

"You're welcome," her boss said. "What do you think? Do you want to cover more hockey stories?"

Was he asking what she thought he was? "Are you assigning me to the Generals beat full-time?"

Frank nodded. "If you want it. If you think you can handle the likes of Tremblay and his teammates."

It almost sounded like a challenge, which was fine. Maya was used to challenges. She'd been trying to prove herself in a male-dominated profession for years. "I can handle it," she said. Colton Tremblay was arrogant, but from everything she'd read, he backed up his ego with his play on the ice. And if he was smart, he'd recognize he needed to get along with the press, at least if he wanted his stint in San Antonio to be more successful than the one in Montreal. "I'll do it."

"Great," her boss said. "We'll make sure you have all the credentials and full access to the team in time for training camp on Thursday."

Maya had forty-eight hours to turn herself into an expert on hockey and prove to Frank he'd made the right decision. No pressure.

CHAPTER TWO

Maya put a bagel in the toaster and poured herself a cup of coffee. She wanted to just grab something on her way out the door, but she knew that would never fly with her parents.

"That's all you're eating?" Papa predictably asked.

"You need a proper breakfast," Mama chimed in. "Sit down. I will make migas."

"No, Mama." Maya shook her head. She loved the traditional Mexican dish of scrambled eggs, corn tortillas, cheese and chilies, but there was no way her stomach could handle it. Not today. Besides, she'd moved back into the family home because of her mother's failing health. That was supposed to mean Maya helping out more, not Mama doting on her as if she were still a child. "You don't have the energy, and I don't have time. I have to get to work. Training camp starts today."

"What is this training camp?" Mama wanted to know.

Maya sat down and spread cream cheese on her bagel. "It's the first day all the players on the team get together to start preparing for the new season. They have practices and team meetings, things like that." She tried to keep her explanation as simple as possible, knowing her parents didn't care about hockey. She doubted her mother even knew what it was. Soccer, or futból, was Mexico's sport.

Her father frowned. "I don't like you doing this job. It's not proper for a young woman, hanging around these men. Will you be in the locker room?"

"I don't know yet," Maya demurred. No way was she getting into an in-depth discussion of locker rooms with her father. What was she supposed to say? That she'd seen a penis before and it wouldn't make her uncomfortable to see another one, even if it belonged to a superstar like Colton Tremblay? Since most everyone brought cameras into the room these days, she doubted there would be much visible genitalia by the time the locker room was opened up to the press, anyway.

"I know you don't like it, Papa, but I'm a journalist. It's what I do."

"So report the news," he said.

Maya stifled a sigh, knowing it was a no-win argument with him. If she reported the 'news' as he put it, Papa would complain about her being in harm's way if she went to cover a shooting or a robbery. He wouldn't be happy no matter what. "People love sports, and reading about their favorite sports team is news to their fans. It's what I like to do, and this job is a great opportunity for me."

She knew there would be talk that she only got the job because she was a woman, and a Hispanic one at that. There was always pressure for sports bureaus to show they valued diversity. Maya didn't care whether she was hired because she was a Hispanic woman, because she graduated in the top five percent of her class at UT Austin, or because of her experience with the local newspaper. In the end, the only thing that mattered was that she had been hired, and now she had a job to do. She intended to show everyone who read All Sports Today's print and online content that she was a top-notch reporter.

"I know it is, and I am proud of you," Papa said. "You've worked so hard. I just worry."

"And I love you for it," Maya said. She reached over and hugged him, then kissed Mama's cheek. "I love you both. I'll see you tonight. And rest, Mama!"

***

'What did you think of the first day of practice?' 'How does it feel to be named team captain?'

The questions came at Colton like torrents and it was hard to follow them all. Then again, the whole first day of training camp with the Generals passed mostly in a blur, starting with the seven a.m. meeting to now, the four p.m. press conference. He held up a hand. "Just a minute, please. One at a time." Colton knew he had to find a way to get control of these things. As captain, he'd be required to meet with the media after every game, win or lose, pretty or ugly. He couldn't allow press availability to turn into a free-for-all. He had to find a way to get along with these people and get them to like him.

Colton wiped his sweaty brow with a towel and took a gulp of Gatorade. "First, it's an honor to be named team captain, especially as the first captain ever of the Generals. It isn't something I necessarily expected or sought out, but I do view myself as a leader, so when Coach Moreau approached me this morning and asked me to assume the role of captain, I was happy to accept. I look forward to wearing the 'C' on my sweater and it's a job I will take very seriously."

Take that, haters, he thought. If people wanted to dismiss him as nothing more than a party animal and a trouble maker, Colton couldn't stop them. He could, however, prove them wrong. This was a prime opportunity to do. His agent was right. Being traded to a new team might be the best thing that ever happened to Colton.

"I thought the first practice went great. It was nice to meet the guys and get out on the ice…" As Colton relaxed and settled into things, he had the opportunity to scan the room. He recognized a lot of the same faces from his first video press conference two days before, and there were some unfamiliar ones as well. If they were unfamiliar now, Colton knew they wouldn't be for long. Soon, he'd know everyone who regularly covered the Generals beat.

There was one in particular he wanted to know better, and he finally spotted her toward the back. The woman with the silky hair and the dark eyes. She'd come at him the other day with a question about his bad boy reputation, and he'd taken her to be the aggressive, pushy type. Today, though, she stayed quiet, appearing almost unsure of herself. It only intrigued Colton even more, and he nodded in her direction. "Did you have a question?"

"Oh, yes…" She glanced down at her notepad as if flustered, then back at him. "I'm sure San Antonio is quite a bit different than Montreal. I'm just wondering how you're adapting so far and what you think of your new home?"

That was it? Nothing hard-hitting? A question better suited for maybe a women's magazine feature of athletes off the ice? Interesting.

"So far, so good, I guess," Colton said. "I haven't

been in town long and all I've really seen is my hotel room and the team facilities. I've heard great things about your city, though, and I look forward to exploring it more when I have time." He flashed her a smile. "Hopefully I can find myself a good tour guide to help show me around."

***

Maya hurried out of the Generals facility after the press conference. She wanted to make a quick getaway, yet she was in no hurry to go back to the bureau. Not after the way she'd just botched her first official day covering the hockey team. 'How do you like San Antonio so far?' Madre de Dios, what kind of lame question was that? Maya expected that to be the first thing Frank asked when he saw her.

She'd have to do better, no doubt about that. These were the big leagues now. Cowering in the back wouldn't do. Heck, she might not have spoken up and asked a question if Tremblay hadn't prompted her to. And what was up with that? Had he been trying to help her, or embarrass her by singling her out?

"Excuse me, Miss Dominguez? Can you wait up a second?"

Maya's first instinct was to keep walking, but she stopped and turned, finding herself face to face with Colton Tremblay. He was freshly showered, and gone were the backward baseball cap and sweaty team logo T-shirt from the press conference. Now he wore jeans and a crisp button down shirt, his dark hair damp and slicked back. He was one good-looking man, that was for sure. Too bad he was so aware of that fact.

"Yes, Mr. Tremblay?"

"It's Colton, please." He gave her that smile again. The same one from the press conference. The one thousands of women probably swooned over. "You rushed out of the room so fast. I was hoping to have a chance to talk to you."

"About what?"

"That question you asked me."

Great. Did he plan to mock her for her poor job performance? "What about it?" Maya asked defensively.

"Are you a native of San Antonio yourself?" he asked. "A local girl?"

"Yes. Born and raised, and I came back as soon as I finished journalism school." Maya wondered what that had to do with anything. "Why?"

"Well, you wanted to know how I like your city, and I can't tell you. I haven't been anywhere. I haven't seen any of it," he said. "I'd like to change that, and thought maybe you could help. Would you care to join me for dinner?"

"Dinner?" Maya stared at him with what she was sure was a dopey expression. "You mean, like a date?" Immediately, she regretted it. She didn't want to give him any ideas. Especially a man of his reputation.

Colton shrugged. "Well, if you're single and interested, I wouldn't be opposed to calling it that," he said. "If you're married or not interested, we can simply call it dinner. Or even an unofficial press availability, if that makes you more comfortable. All I know is that I put in a long day of practice and I'm hungry. I assume you eat too. So what do you say?"

Maya wasn't sure any of it made her comfortable, but he was right about one thing. "Yes, I do eat. In fact, I'm starving," she said. "And no, I'm not married."

"Does that mean it's a date?" Amusement danced in his brown eyes. It was easy to see why women fell for him.

"I didn't say that. Let's go with just calling it dinner," Maya suggested.

"So that's a 'yes,' then?"

"Yes," Maya said. "I know exactly the place to indoctrinate you to my beloved hometown."

MICHELE SHRIVER

CHAPTER THREE

Maya had no idea what to make of Colton's invitation. Although he said it could be a date, Maya doubted she was the type of woman he normally dated. Then again, did playboys like Colton have a type? She hoped she didn't make a mistake by accepting, but he hadn't been pushy about it. Besides, what harm could it do to get to know one of the players she'd be reporting on a little better?

At any rate, if Colton did hope to call it a date, Maya figured he'd change his mind and lose interest in her pretty quick when she had to call home to tell her parents she wouldn't be there for dinner. No, she wasn't his type of woman at all.

"Sorry about that," she said when she got back to their table. Maya slipped her cell phone into her purse, hoping to avoid further interruptions.

"Work?" Colton asked.

Maya shook her head. "No, family. It probably sounds pathetic, but I had to check in with my parents."

"You still live at home?"

Yes, he definitely thought she was pathetic. He might go running before they even ordered their meal. "Yes and no. I moved out after high school, had my own place all through college and up until about six months ago," Maya explained. "My mother was diagnosed with Fibromyalgia, so I moved back in to help her and my father around the house."

"In that case, it's not pathetic at all," Colton said. "It says a lot about your character and your background and dedication to your family that you'd do that." He picked up his menu. "I want to know more about you, but I want to order food first. You said this is your favorite restaurant. What do you recommend?"

"Everything on the menu," Maya said, only halfway joking. Colton's only guideline about where they ate was that he wanted to become acquainted with something uniquely San Antonio and different from what he'd find in Montreal. Maya had never been to Montreal, or even outside Texas or Mexico, but she was fairly certain one couldn't find true Mexican food there, so she selected Paloma Blanca. "This is widely considered to be the best Mexican food in the city, and unlike so many of the touristy places, it's actually authentic."

Colton's brow furrowed as he scanned the menu, and Maya suspected some of the Spanish words were throwing him off. "I usually get the enchiladas verdes," she said. "Verde means green, and that describes the sauce. They're covered in a sauce made from tomatillos. Those are little green tomatoes." *Sheesh, Maya. Way to ramble.* "And if I'm boring you or insulting your intelligence, please tell me."

"On the contrary, I find it interesting," Colton said. "I'm fluent in French and English, but I don't speak a word of Spanish. One of the things that scared me about this trade was adapting to a completely new culture. I'm here, though, and I want to embrace my new home. Are you fluent in Spanish?"

Maya nodded. "Yes. I'm first-generation American. I was born here, but my mother and father were both born in Mexico," she explained. "We still speak a lot of Spanish at home, so if you want to learn it, I can help." Great. Now she was volunteering her services as a language teacher. Presumptuous much? She didn't even know if he'd want to see her again. Still, it impressed her that he would express an interest in learning more about the culture of his new city. Maybe there was more to this hotshot playboy. He seemed very sincere about giving his best to the team and making the trade work.

"I might take you up on that, starting with this menu. I'm a steak guy, and I see something here about a rib eye, but the rest lost me." Colton smiled, his expression amused. "Care to translate?"

Maya chuckled. She should have suspected he was a steak guy. Most athletes she'd known were. "Sure. Carne asada tampiquena," she said. "It's a rib eye, plus you get a cheese enchilada. Queso is cheese. Let's see. Pico de gallo is a cold salad with diced tomatoes, onions, peppers and seasonings. And four gulf shrimp in a cream sauce made with chipotle peppers." Maya looked up from the menu. "It's a heck of a lot of food, but it's good food. We have great steaks in Texas and get some good shrimp from the Gulf of Mexico. You really can't go wrong."

"Sold. It sounds delicious." Colton held up his hand to signal their server.

***

The decision to invite her to dinner was totally spontaneous. Mingling with the press had never been

Colton's thing. Then again, no member of the press had ever intrigued him quite like Maya Dominguez did and Colton had never been the captain of a team before. A good relationship with the media was suddenly essential. He'd meant it when he said they could treat this as a date or a press availability, or anything in between. Colton knew which he preferred, though. Figuring out Maya was the difficult part.

Dining with a member of the press came with plenty of potential pitfalls, too. "Will it reflect badly on me if I order a beer?" he asked.

After a flicker of hesitation, Maya shook her head. "No. I'm off duty and planned to myself. I recommend Negro Modelo."

Since he'd followed the rest of her recommendations to that point, that's what Colton ordered.

"Were you afraid you'd be headline news for having a drink with dinner?"

"Back home, I would have. Then again, I was a celebrity in Montreal, and everything I did was front page news," Colton said. "I'm hoping things might be a little more low-key here, but I'm afraid my reputation precedes me. You certainly didn't waste any time asking me about it."

"Just doing my job," Maya said. "The reports are out there." She raised an eyebrow. "Are you saying they're untrue?"

"Untrue?" Colon hesitated. No, most had at least some bearing in fact. Especially the ones most responsible for his abrupt ticket out of Montreal. "Exaggerated is probably the better term."

"So you think people in my profession might be prone to exaggeration? Shocking!"

It took him a second to realize she was joking, and soon they were both laughing. Good. She had a sense of humor. Colton could appreciate that. "I can't blame everything on overzealous reporting, though," he said after a minute. "I've made my share of mistakes too. Hopefully eventually I'll be able to live them down. The fresh start with a new team and a new city helps." Along with new press.

Their server set their drinks on the table. Colton noticed the beer was served with a lime and that Maya squeezed lime juice into the bottle and then dropped the lime inside. Interesting, but he did the same before trying the beer. "Hmm. Good." He'd visited Dallas before, on road trips to play the Dallas Stars once each season, so Colton wasn't entirely unfamiliar with Texas, but he'd quickly realized that San Antonio was far more rooted in Mexican culture than Dallas. So far he liked his indoctrination to his new city. He couldn't deny that the company had something to do with that.

"Enough about me, though," Colton said. "Tell me more about you. Your family."

"There's not much to tell. I was raised on hard work, and I worked my way through journalism school. Got a job right after graduation with the local newspaper covering sports. Last year, when the NHL decided to expand into San Antonio, All Sports Today opened a bureau to focus exclusively on local sports. High school, college and professional. I applied and got a job. I started out covering the high schools, mostly football, which is big in Texas. And as of two days ago, I'm officially assigned to cover the Generals." Maya smiled. "Which means you and I will be seeing a lot of each other."

"Yes, I guess we will." And that suited Colton just fine.

***

After dinner, Maya drove Colton back to the training facility to pick up his car. "Here we are," she said, a little reluctant for the evening to end. A meal at Paloma Blanca was always good, and she'd enjoyed the company as well. Just how much she'd enjoyed it scared her a little.

"Thanks. As much as I'd love for you to show me more of your fine city, it will have to be another time," Colton said. "Practice starts at seven tomorrow."

"Which will mean a busy day for me, as well," Maya said. "They work you guys hard."

"Yeah. Coach is tough, but I understand it. We're an expansion team and no one else in the league expects anything from us this season, but the fans here are excited to have us and we want to play hard for them," Colton explained.

Maya nodded, again appreciating his dedication to his sport. "You know, I wasn't sure what to think of you at first, given what I'd read," she said. "But I think you're going to do just fine here and make a great team captain. Who knows, maybe the press will give you more of a break too."

"Maybe." His face suddenly took on a worried expression. "Hey, I hope you don't think that's what this is about... Me, just trying to get in good with the press. I really enjoyed dinner, and you're a very interesting woman," he said. "Not to mention beautiful."

Maya couldn't help but smile at the compliment, even if the direction of the conversation was beginning to concern her. He was a playboy and a sports superstar. She was the working class daughter of Mexican immigrants. And her job was to report on him and his teammates. "Colton..."

"I know. Dangerous territory." He put his hand

on the door handle. "That's why I'm opening this door now rather than trying to kiss you."

Relief came over her when he said he wouldn't kiss her. Not because Maya didn't want him to, but because she did. And she worried she might like it too much. "That's probably for the best. I'm not one of your... what is the word... puck bunnies." She'd read plenty about his exploits with the so-called hockey groupies who hung around arenas after games, hoping to score with the players.

"No, you're definitely no puck bunny, Maya Dominguez. And maybe that's exactly what I like about you." Colton opened the door. "I'll see you tomorrow."

MICHELE SHRIVER

CHAPTER FOUR

Colton was at the training facility bright and early the next day, but he wasn't the first to arrive. His new teammate, Trevor Collison, had already laced up his skates.

"You're here early, man." Colton greeted him with a friendly slap on the back.

"Yeah." Trev smiled, his years evident in the lines around his eyes. "This is the end of the road for me. My last chance to make it with an NHL squad. If not, I'm looking at Europe or the minors."

Colton knew it was true. He was familiar with the story of Trev's career. Pretty much everyone in the hockey community was. Trev possessed slick skating ability, a wicked wrist shot and a predilection for liquor, cocaine and women, though not necessarily in that order. The splendid combination of the first two made him a breakout star when he'd first come into the league ten years before. The potentially lethal combination of the other three led to a flame-out of spectacular proportions, and now Trev was known more for his stints in rehab than his magic with the puck. He'd played for four different squads, most recently Carolina, and with each new team vowed things would be different. They always ended the same way, with Trev's demons getting the better of him and his game.

"When the Hurricanes bought out my contract after last season, I didn't know if I'd get another opportunity," Trev continued. "Thank goodness for league expansion, huh?"

"Guess so." Colton smiled wryly. "We can be the San Antonio reclamation projects." It was a lame attempt at a joke and Colton wasn't surprised when Trev didn't laugh.

"Something like that." Trev took his helmet from his locker stall. "Can I talk frankly with you about something, Tremblay? Teammate to teammate?"

"Sure thing." Colton paused from fussing with his skates and looked at Trev. The older man's face held a serious expression. "What's on your mind?"

"I just want to give you a little advice," Trev began. "It's up to you whether you take it, but I hope you'll listen."

"I'm listening," Colton said. It seemed like everyone was full of advice for him lately.

"Good." Trev nodded. "I see a lot of me when I look at you. Me, after I got dumped by my first team, traded from the Senators to Anaheim. I'd worn out my welcome in Ottawa, sure, and there was speculation that I had some problems off the ice, but my play on it was still elite. Plenty of teams were interested in my services. It was a warning, though. One I should have heeded, but I didn't. I didn't get the message, I thought I was invincible." He shook his head. "Look where I am now. All but washed up. Ironically, back in the same city where

I started my hockey career in the days when the AHL was in town. One last chance to keep a once-promising career from being destroyed by that damn white powder."

The intent of his message was clear and Colton wanted to argue that their situations were completely different. After all, Colton never touched the hard stuff. Sure, he liked night clubs and occasionally hit the booze a little heavy, but drugs? Never. Still, he knew the comparisons were there and it probably took everyone with a problem, Trev included, a little time before they progressed to the hard stuff. "I hear you, man," Colton said.

"I hope so," Trev said. "I like you. You're a hell of a hockey player and I think you have the makings of a good captain. So far you're saying and doing all the right things here, and it sounds like maybe you got the message about cleaning up your act."

"I did, yes. And that's exactly what I plan on doing." Colton managed a smile. "That and making Montreal sorry they gave up on me."

"I'm glad to hear it, because I'd hate to see your career end up like mine." Trev strapped on his helmet and reached for his stick. "I'll see you out on the ice, captain."

Colton watched his teammate leave the locker room, wondering if this time Trev really would get things together. He hoped so, both for Trev's sake and that of the team. If they had any chance of success in their first season, they would need to gel quickly as a group. They couldn't afford anyone bringing them down. Was that what it was like for the leadership group in Montreal? Did they worry Colton would bring them down? It was a sobering thought, and all the more incentive to make the most of this new opportunity.

"Hello, Colton." The heavily-accented voice gave away the speaker before Colton even looked up. Nikolai Brantov, nineteen-year-old Russian phenom and the first draft pick in San Antonio Generals history.

"Hi, Nik. How are you?" Colton asked.

"Good. Fine," Nik answered as he reached for his skates.

The kid spoke little English, and the team had arranged for him to live with a host family in San Antonio to help him learn the language and better acclimate to North America. Colton didn't think that was a bad idea at all, since he was still figuring out how to acclimate to San Antonio himself. He didn't need a host family, though. No. Maya Dominguez would do just fine. And where the hell did that thought come from? Wherever it came from, Colton needed to bury it. He was here to play hockey, not fall for a member of the press corps. Even one as beautiful as the delightful Ms. Dominguez.

"Are you settling in okay? Enjoying it here so far?" Colton asked Nik.

The young Russian nodded. "Yes. The family is very kind to me, and I like the team."

"Great. We're all excited to have you." He gave Nik a good-natured slap on the back. "And I'm happy to have you on my wing." The kid had a great shot and Colton could picture good things for their line. "Get ready, and I'll see you out there."

***

Maya stopped by the bureau in the morning before heading to the training facility. The team scrimmage was scheduled for later, but the players would be skating on their own before the scrimmage was open to the press. It gave Maya a little extra time to study up on some of the other players on the team. As exciting a player as Colton was, he wasn't the whole team and it wouldn't do for Maya to be singularly focused on him. *Even if he is sexy as sin.* She quickly tried to banish that thought from her head. What the hell was wrong with her, anyway? She had a job to do.

"Morning, Dominguez." Frank greeted her as he came into the newsroom. "I wasn't sure I'd see you here this morning."

Maya glanced up from her laptop. "The Generals are scrimmaging at ten thirty," she said. "Just getting a little work done here before heading to the rink."

"Good." Frank spun a chair around and straddled it, leaning over the back. "So the hockey beat is working out okay for you so far?"

"You mean after all of four days?" Maya shrugged. "I think so. I'm enjoying it and trying to learn as much as I can about the team, both the players and the coaches."

Frank nodded and rubbed his goatee. "Uh huh. And does that mean you'll get around to having dinner at Paloma Blanca with all of them, or is that only restricted to hotshot team captains?"

The bluntness of the question took Maya aback. Was she in trouble? And how the heck did Frank know? She cocked her head to the side. "Excuse me? I'm not sure how to take that question."

"You had dinner at Paloma Blanca with Colton Tremblay."

It was a statement, not a question, and Maya couldn't deny it. Besides, she'd done nothing wrong. Had she? "Yes. Is that okay?" If Colton truly thought he'd escaped the intense scrutiny of Montreal and would have more privacy in San Antonio, maybe he needed to rethink that. Apparently news traveled fast here, too, and someone obviously recognized the new star hockey player in town.

"Depends," Frank said, and then sighed. "Look, Maya, you can have dinner with whoever you want. I'm just not sure it's a good idea for it to be athletes you're assigned to cover. If you're getting in over your head, I can see about reassigning you..."

In over her head? Maya bristled at the insinuation. "In other words, don't get personally involved with one of the players, or I might find myself covering the girls' softball team at Holmes High School?"

Frank shook his head as he held up a hand as if to try to make peace. "I didn't say that. I like you, Dominguez, and I like your work. I already told you that. If I didn't, you wouldn't have the assignment you do. I'd like to keep you there, but you have to understand that this guy has a reputation and--"

"One he's trying to change!" And how quickly she jumped to Colton's defense. *Watch it, Maya.* "I'm not 'in over my head,' Frank," she said with forced calmness. "And I have no intention of getting personally involved with an athlete whom I report on, be it Colton Tremblay or anyone else. It was a simple dinner. He doesn't know the city and wanted some advice from a local. We both needed to eat, and surely you'll agree that Paloma Blanca is a great restaurant to take someone to if you want to show off the great food here."

Frank sighed. "It's not about your choice in restaurants."

"I know it's not. Just saying..." Maya glanced at her watch. She had to get going soon if she wanted to see the whole scrimmage, which she did. That and the conversation with her boss was beginning to annoy her. "I would think you'd be pleased that I'm developing a good *working* relationship with the players on the team," she said, trying a slightly different tack. "I know some things about Tremblay now that some of the others don't, and he trusts me." She shut down her computer so she could pack it up. "To sort of answer your question, yes, I plan on learning more about the others on the team, too, though that might not involve dinner." She stood up and put her computer in its case. "I actually thought maybe we could run a little feature on each of the guys, showcasing them in a more personal way. You know, help the city get to know its new hockey team. What do you think?" The idea had just come to her, perhaps in an effort to save face and gain credibility with her boss, and Maya hoped Frank wouldn't shoot it down right away.

"Interesting," he said after a minute. "It might work. I'll think about it."

"Thanks," Maya said. "I have to go."

Her boss nodded. "Good luck today. And I'm glad you know what you're doing."

CHAPTER FIVE

Maya watched the maroon versus silver—named for the team colors—scrimmage with intense focus. It wasn't because she was a huge hockey fan, or even an expert on the sport. She was still learning about hits and blocks and body checks. It didn't take being an expert on the nuances of the game to appreciate the speed and skill of the players as they moved on the ice.

She paid particular attention to three players. Colton, of course. He was the captain and marquee player, and seeing him in something close to game action for the first time, it was easy to see why the Generals organization wanted him in spite of the bad boy reputation he'd earned in Montreal. He skated with so much speed that his jersey flapped behind him. When he scored a goal off a beautiful pass from his linemate, Maya had to bite her bottom lip to keep from cheering out loud. Oh, no. She wasn't in over her head at all. She had everything under control.

The assist on Colton's goal came from another player Maya had set her attention on, a young Russian named Nikolai Brantov. Part of her morning research had centered on Brantov, who'd left his native country for the first time a few months before to play hockey in North America. A local family was hosting him in their home, an arrangement that seemed to Maya like that of a foreign exchange student. Except this was a nineteen-year-old who'd just signed an entry-level contract with an NHL team. If Frank liked her idea to run features on the Generals players, and if the higher ups signed off on it, Nikolai Brantov would be one of the first.

Another would be Trevor Collison, who, as Maya learned this morning, was fresh off a stint in rehab and trying to click with his fifth different NHL team. If Colton had a troubled reputation, it was nothing compared to this guy. Would he be able to make the most of this fresh start, or would he succumb to his addiction again? If Collison had any interest in talking to her, Maya wanted to feature his story in their publication.

Unfortunately, neither Brantov nor Collison were among the players made available to the press after the scrimmage, leaving Maya unable to learn anything about their personalities off the ice or their skill—or lack thereof—in handling the media. Colton, of course, was typically smooth and self-assured as he answered questions from the press.

"It felt great to skate in something resembling a game environment," he said in response to Maya's question about what he thought of the scrimmage. The now-familiar cocky grin formed on his face. "And to get a goal, of course." He looked at Maya. "What about you? Did you enjoy what you saw?"

What? Maya simply stared for a few seconds, flustered and embarrassed. Was he mocking her, or flirting with her? One thing was for sure—Colton was very adept at throwing Maya off her game. "I found it more interesting than practice," she finally answered, meeting his gaze. "Like you and your teammates, though, I think most of us here are anxious for the season to start."

***

Damn it. He'd offended her again. Colton knew as soon as the words were out of his mouth. And who could blame her? Since when did players turn the tables and ask questions of the press? It was a first-class jerk move. So why did he do it? The answer was simple. He did it because Maya Dominguez completely disarmed him, in a way no woman ever had before. Not even the one who almost managed to steal his heart. That fact scared Colton to death. He responded by trying to disarm her, and he succeeded, but he also succeeded in offending her. Only one result was planned.

It once again had him racing after her, trying to stop her before she left the facility. "Maya, wait."

She'd nearly reached her car, and stopped and turned around. "Yes, Mr. Tremblay?"

So they were back to formality? He'd definitely offended her. "I'll never get used to hearing that. Mr. Tremblay is my father, and a very strict man," he said. "It's Colton. I thought we reached that point last night."

"And maybe we shouldn't have," she replied.

Maybe. Probably not. But even though Colton knew they were heading into dangerous territory, he couldn't help but want to go further down that path. "I had a great time last night," he said. "Are you actually going to claim you didn't?"

After a few seconds, she shook her head. "No. I enjoyed it as well."

"You're a good tour guide for your city, and a

39

better dinner companion. And I think you're one heck of a reporter too," Colton said. "In case what happened back in the press room had you doubting that."

"Never." A flicker of anger flashed in her eyes. "You also made a fine dinner companion, and you're a heck of hockey player," Maya said. "Your etiquette in press conferences, however, could use some improvement."

She had him there, no doubt about it. "I won't argue with that. I'm new to this captain and face of the franchise thing, and still learning." Colton hoped he sounded humble. "I apologize if I crossed an imaginary line back there, but my curiosity got the better of me. You intrigue me. I want to learn more about you," he said. "And yes, that means finding out whether you look forward to our game tomorrow."

"I fail to see how it matters to you," she countered. "Look forward to it or not, I'll be in the press box watching it, and I'll file a report after the game."

"Right, I know." Colton nodded. "Like I said, a curiosity thing. We as players like to know what the press truly thinks about us, and we rarely get the chance to find out."

"And is your curiosity now satisfied?" Maya asked.

"A little," Colton said. "I'm glad you're looking forward to the game." He shouldn't care, but it meant something to him. He wanted her to enjoy watching him play the sport he loved. "There's something else you can help me with, though. Another curiosity."

Maya frowned a little. "What's that?"

"I've got some free time tomorrow. We've got a team dinner tonight, then we're free until tomorrow night's game," he explained. They'd been practicing hard, and a little downtime would be nice before they suited up for the first preseason game against the Stars. "A lot of the guys will just sleep all day, and sometimes I like to get a nap in myself, but I think I'll be too pumped tomorrow. I need something to do. I'm hoping you can give some advice. I want to play tourist this time." He smiled. "If I'm a tourist in your city, where should I go?"

She appeared to think about it for a minute, and then asked, "Are you interested in dining and shopping, or history?"

Colton didn't have to think about his answer. "History." It sounded a lot better than shopping.

"In that case, you should visit the Alamo."

"The what?"

"The Alamo," she repeated. "You've never heard of it?"

Colton shook his head. "No, 'fraid not." He hoped she didn't think he was stupid. "Is that bad?"

"It is if you're from Texas, but you're obviously not."

"No. Quebec, actually." He smiled again. "So tell me about this Alamo thing."

"It's the site of a famous battle in the war for Texas's Independence," Maya said, then proceeded to give him a brief run down of the attack on the Alamo Mission by the Mexican army and some guy named Santa Anna.

She spoke with enthusiasm, and he guessed she must be a history buff. "That's interesting," he said, "but aren't you Mexican?"

"Mexican-*American*," she corrected. "I was born here, and we studied Texas history in school. But even my papa, who claims to bleed the green, white and red of the tricolor, can acknowledge it was a good thing that Texas gained its independence."

"Fascinating," Colton said, meaning it.

"If you think so, you should definitely visit the Alamo site on your day off tomorrow."

"Oh, I plan to." That much was a given. "I'm hoping you'll join me."

***

"I beg your pardon?" Maya wasn't sure she'd heard correctly. Okay, check that. She'd heard correctly, she just had a hard time believing what she'd heard. Did this guy know anything about boundaries? It didn't seem like it. One thing was certain—life around Colton Tremblay wasn't dull.

"I'd like you to accompany me on my visit to the Alamo," Colton said.

"You mean as a tour guide?" Maya asked. That had to be it, right?

"Sure," Colton said, "if that's what you want to call it." Mischief flickered in his eyes and it was hard to ignore just how sexy those eyes were. "Or we can call it a date."

A date. Exactly what Maya was afraid of, yet wanted at the same time. "Are you sure that's a good idea?"

"No." Colton shook his head. "In fact, I'm pretty sure that it's not. At the moment, though, I don't care. You intrigue me. I want to know you better. And I think I'd be lost by myself. You *have* been to Alamo before, right?"

He won points for his honesty and for recognizing they were flirting with trouble. If Maya were to be completely frank with herself, she didn't care either. As cocky and infuriating as Colton could be, there was also a sincerity to his words. And he wasn't any dumb jock, either. The idea of spending more time with him very much appealed to Maya. "I was born and raised here," she said. "I've been to the Alamo many times."

"Then you'll make an excellent tour guide," Colton said. "And an even better date, should you choose to call it that." His smile was disarming, but carried a hint of humility too.

"I have to work," Maya said, though the protest was weak.

"Doing what?" Colton challenged. "You must have some downtime tomorrow too, since you'll be working the game?"

So much for that. "Yes, I suppose I do."

"Come on, what do you say?" There was that smile again. "Help a Quebecois out?"

When he put it like that, complete with the subtle accent that Maya found so appealing, it became damn near impossible to say no. Especially since she didn't really want to. "Well, I would hate for you to be lost, not knowing where to go…"

"I would be," Colton said. "Like a fish out of water." The familiar twinkle flashed in his eyes again. "We can't have that, can we?"

"No." Maya finally relented. "We can't. I wouldn't be a very good San Antonian if I left you alone to wander cluelessly around the Alamo. I'll be your tour guide."

"Or my date?" Colton challenged.

"Don't push your luck."

Tour guide, my ass, Maya thought as she drove back to the news bureau. She wasn't fooling herself, and she doubted she was fooling Colton. No, she was pretty certain he saw right through her.

"Hey, Dominguez," Frank greeted her when she walked into the newsroom. "How'd the Generals' scrimmage go?"

"Good." She set her computer case on her desk. "Tremblay's the real deal," she said. "And the Russian kid, Brantov, is definitely someone to watch."

Frank nodded. "Some people are even talking Calder Trophy."

The award for the top rookie in the NHL. Maya nodded. "It wouldn't surprise me. He looked good."

"I talked to the top brass about your idea to run personal features on the players," Frank said. "They're interested."

"They are?" Maya tried to keep her tone level and not display too much excitement or surprise.

"Yes. We'd have to work out some logistics, but I think we'll get the go ahead."

"Wow. That's great." *Especially since I just pulled the idea out of my ass this morning.* "Thanks for pitching it, Frank."

"Thanks for suggesting it," he said. "I'm sorry I accused you of getting in over your head, Dominguez. I was wrong. You obviously know exactly what you're doing."

CHAPTER SIX

Maya stood in the lobby of Colton's hotel. She'd arrived ten minutes earlier than their agreed-upon time, and this was after fussing over her appearance for an hour. All this to be a tour guide at the Alamo? Hardly. Maya could admit the obvious, at least to herself. She was interested in Colton Tremblay on a personal level. Admitting it and knowing how to handle it, though, were two different things.

An elevator chimed, signaling its arrival at the lobby level, and Maya turned in that direction just as Colton stepped off the middle one. He wore jeans and a red golf shirt and his dark hair was slicked back and appeared damp, leaving her wondering whether he used gel in it, or was fresh from the shower. *And what does that matter, Maya? Beyond the fact that you're way too interested in everything about this guy.* He smiled as their eyes made contact. "Ah, there she is. The most beautiful tour guide in all of San Antonio."

Maya felt herself blush. She wished he'd quit saying things like that. It made it harder and harder to adhere to her vow of not getting personally involved with an athlete. "The stories were right about what a smooth operator you are," she said, "but it's a dubious claim from someone who's been here such a short time that he still lives in a hotel." She glanced around the lobby. It was, at least, one of the swankiest hotels in town. "Shouldn't the new team captain be putting down roots?"

"Yeah, you got me there," Colton admitted. "I'm living like a nomad, and I don't really like it. But in my defense, I've only been in town a week and a half, and I've been pretty busy. I actually had an appointment set up today with a real estate agent to see some properties, but I had to cancel when I got a better offer."

"Oh?" Maya raised an eyebrow. "You're really that excited about seeing the Alamo?"

"No," Colton said. "I'm excited about spending more time with you. Although I'm sure the history lesson will be nice as well." He shrugged. "I'll reschedule with the realtor for my next day off. For now, it's suitcases and room service. Unless, of course, I can talk you into joining me for dinner more often."

Again, his forthrightness about his intentions and his interest surprised her a little. It was impossible not to be flattered, but Maya was determined to keep her cool. "I'm glad you're serious about finding a house here. It'll go a long ways toward winning over the fans. They like to know their sports stars have embraced the community," she explained. "It's very convenient that you're staying at this hotel, though. We're only two blocks from the Alamo, so I thought we could walk, if that's okay?"

Colton nodded. "Fine with me. It's supposed to be a nice day. Shall we?" he asked, as he reached for her hand.

"Is this a Canadian thing? Holding hands with your tour guide?" Instead of pulling her hand away, though, Maya linked her fingers through his.

"You're the one insisting you're merely my tour guide," Colton reminded her. "As far as I'm concerned, you're my date. And what kind of date would it be if I didn't hold your hand? We Canadians *do* have a reputation for being unfailingly polite."

***

It surprised Colton that Maya didn't rebuff his attempt to take her hand, as determined as she was in insisting there would be nothing personal between them. She could insist all she wanted, but her actions belied her words. She was interested. She just may not have admitted it to herself yet.

As they strolled hand-in-hand down the block, Colton was struck by how different Maya was than any other woman he'd ever known. For one thing, he would have gotten the others in his bed by now. Or if he hadn't, he would have grown bored of them and moved on to another who wouldn't make him wait so long. After all, he was a professional hockey player. There would always be women ready and willing to share his bed. Even here, on an expansion team that had yet to play an actual game, the puck bunnies were already forming lines outside the facility. It never took them long.

Yes, there were willing women. Easy women. And for the first time in his life, Colton had ignored them all, instead setting his sights on a woman who excited him and fascinated him, but who insisted she was unattainable.

47

"You're surprisingly quiet," Maya observed, interrupting the silence.

"Yeah, just thinking," Colton said. *About you.*

"Well, we're here." Maya pointed at an aged stone building.

"This is the Alamo?" The building didn't seem all that large, but then again, he hadn't really had any idea what to expect in terms of the size.

"This whole area comprises the Alamo complex." Maya gestured to their surroundings. "We can go inside in a minute and I'll show you the church and the long barracks, but there's something else I want to show you first." She led him to the left of the plaza in the direction of the U.S. Post Office.

Huh? "I realize I'm Canadian, but I have seen a post office before," Colton said with a chuckle.

"Yes, but not this one." Maya stopped near the front of it. "This is believed to be the site where William Barret Travis was killed in the final assault. He was a lieutenant colonel in the Texas Army, and he died fighting to the bitter end. See this?" Maya pointed at a plaque on the ground, "This is the text of a letter he sent to the people of Texas."

Colton had to bend down a little in order to clearly make out the inscription on the monument, which spoke of being besieged and the enemy's demand for full surrender and ended with the words 'Victory or Death.' "And in his case, it was obviously death."

Maya nodded. "Yes, but this letter, this rally cry, was a motivator for the Texas army, and for the rest of the United States, really, to fight harder for Texas' Independence."

She spoke the words with passion, as if she believed them, which surprised and intrigued him even more, given that she appeared to embrace her Mexican heritage with the same passion. Then again, maybe it shouldn't surprise him. As a French-Canadian, Colton embraced the history of both. And perhaps Maya was a woman who approached everything with passion and intensity. Colton was sure of one thing. He wanted to find out. "Very intriguing," he said, referring more to his companion than the heroic Commander Travis.

"Then you'll like the rest of the monument too," Maya predicted. "Let's go inside."

Colton walked with her back to the stone building and reached for his wallet, prepared to pay an admission fee. It turned out he didn't need it. "There's no charge?"

"Oh, you can pay for guided tours if you'd like," Maya explained. "But it's free to wander around on your own, and besides, you have the best tour guide in town, isn't that what you said?"

"Yes, I did. And so far, you're proving me right." Colton returned his wallet to his back pocket. "How do they keep the place going, though, if they don't charge admission?"

"The gift shop," Maya said. "We can go in there if you want to. They have books and souvenirs, and also fudge that's better than pretty much anything else in the world."

"Oh, I doubt that's possible," Colton said.

"It is. Wait until you try it."

"I'll definitely try it," he promised. "I just think you're probably overstating its greatness. I doubt a piece of fudge can be better than sex, for example."

Her cheeks reddened a little, but the blush was accompanied by a smirk. "Then maybe you're about to be surprised."

***

What the heck was she doing, flirting with him? She needed to stop before this thing between them, this whatever it was, went any further. So far, their visit to the Alamo had not gone according to Maya's plan.

She expected Colton to be disinterested. After all, he was a sports star, and a Canadian one to boot. What interest could he possibly have in a shrine to the Texas Revolution? For a history buff like Maya, it remained a fascinating place, no matter how many times she'd been there, and her interest was even greater because of her Mexican ancestry. But Colton? She figured he would be bored out of his mind. Of course he would be, and then she would know they had nothing in common and couldn't possibly have a personal relationship.

Except Colton seemed genuinely interested in the Travis plaque by the post office, and the interest carried over when they got inside the building and Maya showed him the Sacristy.

"So this is where women and children sought protection during the battle," he observed, reading the sign in the small, inner room of the Alamo church.

"Yes. After the last stand, they were found hiding here."

Colton rapped a fist against the three foot thick wall. "Definitely solid. I can see how it would be considered one of the safest places."

He continued to express interest and pepper her with questions as they toured the Long Barrack. "They've really done an excellent job restoring everything, yet still maintaining the rich history," he said.

"Are you sure you're not bored yet?" Maya challenged.

Colton shook his head. "Not bored at all. I do want to check out the gift shop though, maybe find something for my mother." His lips curled in a half-smirk. "And of course, sample that fudge you boasted about."

A gift for his mother. Good grief. How was she supposed to avoid falling for him when he said things like that? Maybe he was kidding.

He wasn't kidding. Instead, he picked a blown glass Christmas ornament featuring the Alamo facade. "She collects Christmas ornaments," he explained.

"Then I'm sure she'll like that." So the bad boy hockey player had a soft spot for his mother. As close as she was to her own mother, Maya couldn't help but appreciate that. More points for Colton. He kept racking them up.

"Now where's this famous fudge that you insist I have to try?"

He obviously wasn't letting that one go, making Maya wish she'd never brought it up. "Right over here," she said, and led him to the counter, where she asked for two samples and then held one out to him before popping the other in her mouth. She already knew she'd purchase a pound of the fudge, but never resisted a free sample.

"Mmm. Definitely good," Colton said. "Maybe not better-than-sex good, but very good."

"I might have been a little bold in my assessment," she admitted.

"Or having some less than spectacular sex," Colton countered, the now-familiar smirk appearing again.

Maya felt her cheeks redden. "I am not even going there with you."

Colton nodded. "Yes. I expected you to say that." He touched a finger to his upper lip. "You've got a speck of fudge right there," he said, but before Maya could lick it or brush it off, his lips met hers in a kiss.

Every rational, intelligent bone in her body cautioned her to push him away. Instead, Maya parted her lips in response. His tongue tasted of the fudge they'd just sampled, as she knew hers must as well, and the sensation was incredibly appealing. Her breathing was irregular when Colton finally broke the kiss.

"It's gone now," he said with a grin. "And I think I'm beginning to see how the fudge can be an aphrodisiac, even if it itself isn't better than sex."

Arrogant. He was so damn arrogant. And so damn sexy. "You shouldn't have done that," Maya said.

"Kiss you? Oh, believe me, I know that. But I wanted to, and I think you wanted it too."

If he expected her to admit that, he was mistaken. "It can't happen again. I'm a reporter. And you're a player. In more ways than one," she added.

Colton blinked, leaving her wondering if she'd offended him. "Right on one and a half counts," he said. "I play hockey, yes. And in the past, I've been guilty of playing games with women. But this, Maya? What's happening between us? This is no game I am playing."

CHAPTER SEVEN

Try though he might he might to get Maya—and that kiss—out of his head in order to get some rest before the game, it was impossible. Every time he started to drift asleep, thoughts of her invaded in his mind. And they were dangerous thoughts. The afternoon spent at the Alamo, culminating in the kiss, had changed nothing. Or maybe it changed everything. The only thing Colton knew for sure was that he wanted her more than he'd ever wanted any woman. He also knew he'd have to work harder than he'd ever worked to get her. That was fine. He liked challenges.

Predictably, Maya had closed up after the kiss. Gone was the fun, even a little flirtatious companion who'd shown him around the monument with passion and intelligence. She was replaced by the efficient, all-business reporter. She wanted to buy her fudge and be on her way. She had work to do to get ready for the game that night. Didn't he?

Since he did want to take a little pre-game nap,

they walked the short distance back to his hotel in relative silence and parted in front of the revolving door to the lobby. She had, at least, wished him good luck. It meant a lot to Colton because he knew she wasn't speaking as a reporter when she said it. Would she be able to turn that sentiment off tonight when she watched the game from the press box?

With the nap a lost cause, Colton reported to the arena early, dressed in his best suit and tie. He passed by Coach Moreau's office on the way to the locker room, not surprised to find the head man already there. Colton stuck his head in. "Hey, Coach."

The older man looked up. "Hi, Colton. You're early."

He nodded. "Yeah. Too wound up, I guess."

"You're not the only one," the coach said. "Collison's already in the locker room. I'm glad you're here. There's something I want to run past you."

"What's that?" Colton leaned against the door frame, hands in his pockets.

"New line combination. Just something I thought about after yesterday's skate, and if we're going to try it, preseason is the time." Coach Moreau looked at him. "I'm moving Collison up to your left wing," he said. "Brantov will still be on your right. I like the way Collison's been skating, and I want to see if he has top-line potential left in him. You okay with that?"

As if Colton had a choice? "You're the coach. I'll play with anyone you put on my line," he said. "I agree, though. Trev's looked good." Maybe the guy really could turn things around this time. "I think Nik and I have developed some good chemistry together, and Trev's got some sniping ability. Let's see how it works." He liked the potential, for sure.

"Great." Coach smiled. "Go get ready. I'll be down in a little bit."

Colton made his way to the locker room and sure enough, Trev was already there. He'd changed from the suit the players were required to wear to the arena and sat in front of his locker in shorts and a Generals T-shirt, his head down as if deep in thought.

"You okay, man?" Colton asked.

Trev looked up and nodded. "Just a little nervous. First game, last chance," he said. "Did you see Coach?"

"I did." Colton tugged his tie off and draped it over a hook in his locker. "Heard about the change. I'm ready to play with you and see what you can do."

"I'll try not to let you down."

"I'm not worried," Colton said. No, he was more worried about himself and playing in front of Maya. "I've got a lot on the line here too. You never know. Maybe I'll let *you* down."

Trev gave him a half-smile. "I doubt that will happen. You seem to be making the most of the fresh start and really towing the line here."

Colton hung his suit coat in the locker and unbuttoned his shirt. "Trying to." Well, except for the part about letting himself get too close to a certain very beautiful reporter. "Hey, Trev. You're single, right?"

"Yeah. Was married, but she couldn't handle my issues. Divorced me a couple years ago."

"Sorry about that."

Trev shook his head. "It's my own fault. I suck at relationships. Always have." He exhaled sharply. "Did you know I first fell in love in this town, back in the AHL days?"

"She the one you married?" Colton asked.

"No. She's just the one I'll always love."

"Ouch. She still in town?"

"Don't know," Trev said. "I doubt it. Not that it matters. Danielle was pure class, and I wasn't enough for her then. No way would I stand a chance now."

"Don't sell yourself short," Colton said. His teammate's words got to him, though. Did a womanizing party boy, even one who was trying to reform, stand any chance with a woman like Maya Dominguez?

"Hey, why are you suddenly so interested in my love life?" Trev asked with a chuckle. "Were the rumors about you and Jana McLean true?"

Even accompanied by the laugh that indicated Trev was merely teasing, the question made Colton freeze up. "Word of advice, Collison. If you want to get along as my wing mate, don't *ever* mention that name to me again."

***

Maya took her seat in the press box, surrounded completely by men, and tried not to let her nerves get the better of her. Not only was she the only woman on the press team, she was covering her first ever hockey game. Oh, and she'd kissed the team's captain and star player just a few short hours ago. If Maya was any further in over head, she might drown.

The kiss had been so good that Maya didn't want it to stop. Instead, it was up to Colton to put a stop to things, which thankfully he had, because otherwise Maya didn't know how far it would have gone. Okay, since they were standing in the middle of the Alamo gift shop at the time, hopefully not too much further. Still, they'd been so close to his hotel... *Stop it, Maya.* Fortunately, Colton halting things had prompted her brain to start functioning again. She had a game to get ready for, and so did he. Nothing like that could ever happen again, no matter how good it might have felt.

"Well, well, well. Maya Dominguez." A familiar voice interrupted her thoughts of Colton's lips on hers, and she turned around.

"Shaun Stanton." They'd been in journalism school together and even dated for a while, but competing for the same position with college newspaper—a position Maya ultimately got—put an end to that. Maya hadn't seen Shaun since graduation. "What brings you here?" He had press credentials hanging on a lanyard around his neck, but Maya had never seen him at any of the team press conferences before.

Shaun slid into the seat beside her and gave her an easy smile. "I'm writing for a hockey-related blog. Just got creds today," he said, holding up his credential. "So I guess you can say I'm the new kid on the block."

"I thought that was me," Maya said with a chuckle. It was nice to not be the most inexperienced member of the press beat. Except Shaun ran a hockey blog, which meant he must know a lot about the sport and the players, as where the only expertise Maya could claim was that the captain was a really good kisser.

"Nonsense," Shaun said. "I've been following your career, Maya, and I'm pretty impressed. From the local newspaper to All Sports, and now your own beat. Not bad at all, especially for a woman."

"What's that supposed to mean?" Maya asked, suddenly feeling a little defensive. She'd never really taken Shaun for a chauvinist.

He shrugged. "Just that it's largely a male-dominated profession, and you seem to have broken through. Congratulations. I always figured you'd do well."

"Thanks, Shaun." Now he sounded a little more like the guy she once dated.

"So, since you were around for camp and the

scrimmage, what's your take on the team so far?" Shaun set his laptop on the table in front of them.

"I think they have potential," Maya said. "I hear Collison is skating on the top line with Tremblay and Brantov tonight. That should be interesting."

Shaun nodded. "They'll need his speed if they want to keep up with Dallas," he said. "I think Collison's the wild card this year. Could be a great signing, if he can keep from snorting the white powder up his nose. Granted, that's a big if. Then there's Tremblay—"

"What about him?" Maya interrupted.

"Another potentially great player, assuming he can keep from sticking his dick where it doesn't belong."

Maya sucked in a breath. She knew Colton had a reputation, but she wasn't prepared to hear it referenced quite so crudely. Then again, Shaun hadn't minced words when it came to Trevor Collison, either. Was he writing for a hockey blog, or a gossip column? "He's been the consummate pro since he arrived in San Antonio." There was she was, jumping to his defense again. "He really seems to welcome the fresh start."

"Good for him." Shaun snorted. "It'll certainly be interesting to see what happens when he goes back to Montreal. First game of the regular season, he goes back to his old playground to see his former mates. Man, you can't script it any better than that. I wish I could be there for that one."

"You're not traveling to the game?"

Shaun shook his head. "Probably not. Small operation. No budget for that. You?"

"Yes. I'll be traveling to all of the road games."

Shaun whistled. "Nice," he said. "You'll have to tell me if there are any fireworks."

"Why would there be?" Maya asked.

"Well, you know...Tremblay made a few enemies before he got run out of town. They may not be so happy to see him again."

***

The crowd. The 'Meet your Generals' video they played on the Jumbotron. The sound of the goal horn, followed by the song played over the arena's sound system when he scored the game-winning goal. Colton relished it all, every bit of it. It may have been only a preseason game, but the atmosphere was great. No, it wasn't the Bell Centre in Montreal and a fan base used to Cup glory, but the arena was packed, the crowd was into the game, and as a team, they'd fed off the energy and gotten the victory.

"The vultures will be here in two minutes." The voice of the team's media liaison reverberated through the locker room. "Make sure you keep your clothes on. Remember, we have a female on the beat."

"Yeah, Tremblay's getting to know her real well too."

Colton turned in the direction of the teammate who'd made the remark. Naturally, it came from Seth Rollins. It seemed like every team had a guy who thought they were funny when they weren't, and on this team, it looked to be Rollins. "I'm the captain. It's part of my job to get along with the press. You got a problem with that?"

"No," Rollins said. "No problem."

Colton hoped the loudmouth veteran defender meant it. He didn't want any issues in the locker room.

The door opened, and suddenly the reporters were there. Cameras were on him and mics and recording devices were shoved in his face as the questioning began. Colton stood in front of his locker as he faced them.

"I thought it was a great atmosphere out there," he said in response to the first question. "The crowd seemed to be into it and it makes me excited for the regular season to start."

"And how do you feel about going back to Montreal for the season opener?" The question came from Maya.

"I look forward to it. It's a chance to show the Canadiens what they lost when they traded me and maybe make them regret it a little bit." Colton couldn't help it. He was a competitor and he had an ego. Naturally, he wanted them to see they made a mistake.

"It's also my hometown, of course, and a chance to play in front of my family and friends." He looked at Maya, wanting to ask her if she was part of the press corps going to Montreal. Colton hoped so. He wanted to show her around his city much the same way she'd shown him around hers. He didn't dare ask, though. He'd crossed the line once before. He wasn't stupid enough to do it again.

Colton shifted his gaze to another reporter, awaiting their question. Before it came, he heard a whistle to his left. Or was it a cat call?

"Hey, Miss Dominquez? What do you think of our locker room?" Sure enough, it was Rollins. Colton turned his head just in time to see him grab his crotch. "Were you hoping to see some of this?"

"Jesus, Rollins. Shut the fuck up." Colton wanted to shove him in a locker stall, but he held back. He didn't want Maya to think all hockey players were assholes. No, just Rollins. "Show a little class, okay? You know, if you can."

He turned back to face the press group. "Sorry about that, everyone. It seems someone forgot his manners." It was directed to all of them, but his his eyes met Maya's. If she was embarrassed, she didn't show it.

"That's all right. I've known rude and crude men before, and seen genitalia as well. I doubt he has anything there that will shock me too much." Then she smiled. She actually smiled. "Or impress me, either."

Colton stared, feeling gobsmacked. It was official. Maya Dominguez was one cool customer. And he might be falling just a little bit in love with her.

CHAPTER EIGHT

After a few more questions, the press was ushered out of the locker room, presumably so that the guys could shower. And Seth Rollins could play with himself.

"What an ass," Shaun muttered under his breath as they left.

"I couldn't agree more," Maya said. Though she'd been telling the truth when she said she wasn't particularly shocked or offended by his gesture, she'd made the decision that Rollins would not be one of the players she spotlighted in the paper and on the All Sports website, assuming the editor-in-chief did approve the feature. And if someone higher up wanted to include him, Maya would not do the interview.

"I mean, seriously. Does he think he just because he wears the 'C' now that he's the moral police and can call other people on the carpet for their actions?" Shaun let out a laugh. "Sounds like someone's getting a little too big for his hockey britches."

"What are you talking about?" Because clearly

they were talking about two different things.

"Tremblay, of course. Comes here, gets named captain, and suddenly we're supposed to believe he's some good, upstanding guy out to protect the only woman on the press corps from the likes of his less-civilized teammate?" Shaun shook his head. "Unbelievable."

"What's 'unbelievable' is anyone, least of all you, thinking I need protecting from anyone." Maya bristled. "I don't need protecting. I don't need to be coddled. Colton knows that."

"Colton?" Shaun raised an eyebrow. "So you're on a first name basis with this guy?"

"I didn't say that." First Frank, now Shaun. Once again, Maya was left backpedaling. She'd have to be more careful with her words.

"I hope you're not getting sucked in by this guy's charm, Maya."

She was getting sick and tired of people warning her about Colton. Especially since she probably knew him better than any of them. How much time had Shaun spent with him? Ten minutes, in a crowded locker room with the rest of the press corps. So now he was an expert? Maya sent Shaun a glare. "Have I ever struck you as the type of woman that got 'sucked in' by a guy's charm?"

After a second, Shaun shook his head. "Not mine, anyway. Or at least not for very long. You were always too interested in your career, even back in J-school." He smiled at her. "Eyes on the prize. You never strayed from what you wanted."

"That's right," Maya said. "I don't make apologies for it. It's hard for a woman in this profession. I have to work to be the best. And yes, that started in J-school."

"Which explains why you never really had time

for me back then," Shaun said. "What about now, though? Now that you've made it to the top, NHL beat for an all sports publication.... any time for a lowly blogger like me?" he asked. "Care to join me for a post-game drink or a late dinner?"

Maya hesitated. Shaun might be an old friend from J-school, but there was something about his behavior and his remarks tonight that didn't sit quite right with her. She also wasn't interested in rekindling what they'd shared in the past, which hadn't been all that great to begin with, and didn't want to lead him on.

Fortunately, before she could answer, the door to the Generals' locker room opened and the team's media liaison stepped out. "Ms. Dominguez? Glad I caught you. I have a note for you." He handed her a slip of paper.

Maya suspected who it was from before she unfolded it.

Don't leave. I want to see you. C.

Colton was asking her to wait for him, which Maya wanted to do. But she had the Shaun problem to deal with.

He raised an eyebrow and nodded toward the note in her hand. "What's that about?"

None of your business. "Oh, just trying to coordinate some player interviews my publication has planned." She hoped it sounded convincing and Shaun wouldn't question why the media liaison would hand her a note about that rather than call the editor-in-chief.

Shaun nodded. "Of course. You've hit the big time now." Was it Maya's imagination, or was there a trace of jealousy in his tone? "So what about that drink, big shot?"

This time there was no hesitation. "No, thank you," Maya said. "I have to get back to the bureau and finish my report."

"Maybe some other time," Shaun said. "I'll walk out with you, though."

"You go ahead. I need to use the restroom." Hopefully he wouldn't wait for her. "It was nice running into you again, Shaun." She turned around and darted into the nearby ladies' room, glad to be away from him but unsure exactly why she felt relieved.

Maya studied her reflection in the mirror before pulling her lipstick from her bag for a touch- up. Great. Now she was checking herself in the mirror and refreshing her make up before seeing Colton, all the while trying to insist to him that their relationship had to stay purely professional. Who the hell did she think she was fooling? That line had already been crossed.

When she pulled open the door of the restroom, there was no sign of Shaun. Colton stood leaning against the wall by the locker room door, dressed in a suit and tie, his hair damp from the shower. He looked even more gorgeous than usual, if that were possible. "Hi," Maya said, trying to ignore the little flutter her heart did.

Colton smiled at her. "Thank you for waiting."

"You said you wanted to see me. I hope you don't think you need to apologize again for your teammate's crass behavior."

"No." He shook his head. "I know you're more than capable of taking care of yourself and don't need me looking out for you," he said. "I simply wanted to see you."

"Okay, you're seeing me." She chastised herself inwardly for resorting to rudeness again. It never seemed to have the effect of scaring Colton away, and besides, she didn't really want to.

"Yes, and I'd like to see a lot more of you,"

Colton said, "and I don't mean at press conferences. I meant what I said this afternoon. I'm not playing a game with you, Maya. What can I do to prove that to you?"

His tone was earnest, and he kept wearing down her defenses. Still, if he was serious, Maya had one more test. "You want to prove yourself? Come to dinner at my house. Meet my family."

She expected a protest. It was too soon. He wasn't ready for that. Instead, Colton's eyes lit up. "I'd enjoy that very much. I'd like to meet them."

"You say that now." Would he still say that after he *had* met them? "My older brother will be there. He's a police officer."

"As far as I know, I don't have any arrest warrants," Colton said, undeterred. "I look forward to meeting him."

Maya tried again. "My father can be very overprotective," she said. "He once went after one of my dates with a shotgun."

Colton's lips twitched in a smile. "Then I'll do my best not to rile him up."

He was determined, that's for sure. "Fine, then, you can come," Maya said. "I'll have Mama make a traditional Mexican delicacy for you to try. Lengua." She smiled.

"What's that?"

"Beef tongue." Surely that would do that. He'd be backtracking now, scrambling for an excuse, any excuse. "From a cow. Mama makes the best tacos de lengua."

***

Tacos made with cow's tongue. The thought had Colton blanching a bit, but he detected the hint of a smirk on Maya's face. Was she merely testing him? Colton had a hunch that was the case, and it was a test he intended to pass.

"I've never eaten tongue before, in tacos or otherwise." Nor did he want to, but for Maya, he'd do it, if that's what it took. "I'm anxious to try it," he said, trying to force sincerity into his tone.

Maya stared at him for a few seconds before she laughed. "No, you're not."

"Really, I am. It sounds delicious." Now he was laughing too. "Or...not."

"Once you acquire a taste for it, it is," Maya said, still laughing. "It's definitely an acquired taste, though."

"Do I really have to acquire it in order to see you again?" Colton asked. *Please, no.*

Maya shook her head. "No. You passed. We'll make carne asada," she said. "Grilled steak, as you might recall from our previous dinner."

Colton smiled, relieved. "Yes, I remember. Much more to my liking." He exhaled. "You almost had me there, but the smirk gave it away. You were testing me."

"Yes," she admitted. "And like I said, you passed. With flying colors."

"Great," he said. "So what day are we doing this?"

"When's your next day off?"

Colton thought for a minute. They were going to St. Louis tomorrow, then Chicago before coming back to San Antonio to play Colorado. "A week from Wednesday. After the preseason. We get a little break before heading to Montreal."

"A week from Wednesday it will be, then," Maya said.

It seemed like forever to Colton, but at least he'd still see her at press conferences. He wanted more, though. "What are you doing now? Can I interest you in a late dinner?"

Not surprisingly, she shook her head. "No. Your work may be done, but mine's not. I have to get to the bureau."

Colton expected as much, and didn't press. Instead, he tipped his head down to kiss her forehead. "Okay, then. Don't work too hard."

He expected her to stiffen, pull away, and tell him he shouldn't do that, but instead she merely smiled. "I won't. I'll see you later, Colton. And great game tonight, by the way."

"Thank you," he said. He watched her walk down the hall, toward the press exit, before picking up his bag. He slung it over his shoulder and headed to the players' exit.

They were waiting outside. The groupies, or puck bunnies, and once they saw him, they screamed and whistled his name.

"Hey, Colton, want some action tonight?" One of them, a particularly busty blonde, asked. "Blow jobs are my specialty."

She wasn't shy, that's for sure. And hey, everyone had to be good at something. "Not tonight," Colton said and began the solitary walk to his car.

CHAPTER NINE

Although she saw Colton every day, their interactions over the past week and a half were limited to work. The Generals went three and two in their preseason games, leaving nearly everyone in San Antonio looking forward to the start of the regular season, which would come Saturday in Montreal. Maya's travel for the Montreal game, as well as the one the next night in Ottawa, was booked and she was both nervous and excited about the opportunity to travel to Canada for the first time and to see Colton's hometown. Were there any special sites he wanted her to see, and more importantly, would they have the opportunity to see them together?

Don't get ahead of yourself, Maya. He might not want anything more to do with you after he meets your crazy family. As much as she'd looked forward to this dinner, Maya also wondered if she'd made a huge mistake. Since her inviting a man to the house for dinner and to meet her family was such a rare occurrence, naturally Mama went overboard and wanted to prepare a feast to rival that of the Virgin of the Guadalupe. And with her mother's deteriorating health, that meant Maya herself had to make much of the food, including the tacos de lengua. There would also be carne asada and pork tamales, but Maya wondered if Colton would be brave enough to sample the lengua.

As she measured lard to make the refried beans, her brother came to stand beside her. "Tenemos que hablar, hermana."

We need to talk. Maya had a hunch what it was about. She turned the heat down on the stove and turned to face Rafael. "Que, Rafa?" If he was going to address her in Spanish, then she would use the Spanish nickname she knew he didn't like. No, he much preferred the Americanized 'Rafe,' much to Papa's displeasure.

"In private," Rafe said, and pointed in the direction of Maya's room.

Maya followed Rafe down the hall. "What?" she asked again, in English this time.

Her brother towered over her by a good six inches. At least he wore civilian clothes and not his uniform. Even if he was off-duty, Maya wouldn't have put it past Rafe to dress in his police uniform merely to try to intimidate her date.

"You don't often bring men home to meet the family," Rafe said.

"Not after Papa went after Jose Cruz with his shotgun you mean?" Maya asked with a laugh. At least she could laugh about it now. At the time, she'd been mortified. She never saw Jose again. "Do you blame me?"

Rafe's lips turned upward. "No. That's why this invitation surprised me. This guy. This hockey player. Is he special?"

Maya considered the best way to answer. "I don't know yet, Rafe. We're still getting to know each other. He's different, though. Completely different than anyone else I've ever dated. And not just because he's a famous athlete and Canadian." No, there was more to it than that. There was something about the way Coltom made her feel. Maya wasn't ready to go into details about that with her over-protective brother, though.

"And your job?" Rafe asked. "I can't imagine it's a good idea for you to have a personal relationship with an athlete you're assigned to report on."

Leave it to Rafe to get right to the heart of the matter. Maya shook her head. "Not really, no. It's..." she searched for the right word "...frowned upon." *To say the least.*

"So your job might be in jeopardy?"

Again, Maya hesitated. She didn't want to think about that. No, there had to be options. Options that didn't involve her covering the Generals anymore. "I suppose it could be," she admitted. More likely, though, she'd be reassigned. She'd have a job; it just wouldn't be the one she'd dreamed of.

"And is this guy worth it? Is he worth sacrificing what you've worked so hard for?" Rafe's tone was skeptical.

"I don't know, Rafa," Maya admitted. "I'm still figuring that out. Can you do me a favor, though?"

"What's that?"

"Give him half a chance."

***

Colton parked in front of a well-maintained home in a middle class neighborhood and double-checked the address Mays had given him. Yes. This was the place. It was time to meet her family. The police officer brother, shotgun toting father and a mother whose culinary specialty was the tongue of a cow. What exactly was he getting himself into? An evening with the most interesting—and one of the most beautiful—women he'd ever met. And Colton had met a lot of women in his life.

He'd spent the afternoon fretting over what to bring, if anything. Etiquette dictated he bring something, and his French mother would naturally suggest a bottle of wine. Wine, though, didn't seem to be a natural pairing with Mexican food. Beer seemed too informal, and besides, what if Maya's family didn't drink alcohol? She had mentioned her mother suffering some health problems. He finally settled on fresh flowers. Two bouquets. One for Maya and one for her mother. Hopefully that wasn't out of line.

Colton rang the doorbell and Maya answered it, wearing an orange knee-length, sleeveless dress that complemented her natural coloring. She looked beautiful, as always, and he wanted to kiss her. Instead, he merely greeted her with a smile. "Hi."

"Hi, yourself. Did you have difficulty finding the house?"

"No. Your directions were fine." As well as the GPS on his car. "These are for you." Colton held out one of the flower bouquets.

"Thank you. They're lovely." The hint of a blush came over her cheeks. "Please, come in. I'll introduce you to everyone."

Colton followed her into the house and was hit right away with delightful aromas emanating from the kitchen. "Wow. It smells wonderful in here."

"I hope you're hungry," Maya said. "I teased Mama about preparing a spread suitable for the feast of the Virgin of Guadalupe."

"I have no idea what that is," Colton admitted. "I'm guessing it involves a lot of food, though."

"It's a feast in December to honor Mexico's

patron saint." Maya chuckled. "And yes, it involves a lot of food." She led him into the kitchen. "Mama, Papa, Rafael, this is Colton Tremblay. Colton, this is my father, Miguel Dominguez."

Colton nodded at the older man and extended his hand. "Nice to meet you, sir." *I hope you kept your shotgun safely put away.*

Mr. Dominguez said something in Spanish that Colton didn't understand, but since the man shook his hand, he figured it wasn't too horrible.

"My mother, Rosa Dominguez," Maya continued with the introductions.

She was pleasantly plump, probably from eating her own delicious cooking. "A pleasure." Colton held out the other bouquet of flowers. "I brought these for you."

The woman's tired eyes lit up. "Muy gracias." During his three-and-a-half weeks in San Antonio, Colton had picked up enough Spanish to know Maya's mother had thanked him, but as she turned to Maya and said something else, Colton was left in the dark about the translation.

"So far you're winning points with my parents," Maya's brother said, stepping forward and extending a hand. "I'm Rafe, Maya's brother."

The man's handshake was firm. "Hi. Maya tells me you're a police officer."

"That's right."

"I have an uncle that serves on the provincial police force in Quebec," Colton said.

"So that's where you're from? Quebec?" Rafe asked.

"Yes, Montreal."

"And you play hockey."

"Yes." Colton smiled. "I'm Canadian, which

basically means I've been skating as long as I've been walking."

"In Mexico, children kick futbóls soon after they walk," Maya's father said.

"I've heard that, yes," Colton said. "I've never played soccer, but I have watched it. It has some similarities to hockey." He thought it was true enough, and hoped he hadn't offended Mr. Dominguez with the comparison.

"Are you hungry?" Mrs. Dominguez asked. "We should eat. I made tacos de lengua."

Of course. "Sounds delicious." Colton exchanged a glance with Maya. If he was still being tested, he intended to pass. "I've never had lengua before, but Maya assures me it's delicious."

***

Maya relaxed a little as they sat down to eat. Colton's manners were impeccable. He'd even brought her mother flowers. And he was a good sport in agreeing to try the tacos de lengua. Assuming he didn't cough, gag or spit it out, he'd probably make a good impression with her parents. *Please, don't spit it out.*

She shouldn't have worried. Although Colton did reach for his water glass to take a drink after sampling the lengua, he nodded his head in apparent approval.

"Not bad," he said. "It's actually very tender."

Mama turned to Maya and beamed. *'Me cae bien. Él tiene buen gusto.'*

He has good taste. Maya wondered if her mother referred to Colton's taste in food or in women. Either way, he seemed to be winning Mama over.

"How do you like San Antonio so far?" Rafe asked him.

"I've been so busy I haven't seen as much of it as

I'd like," Colton said. "But what I have seen, I like. It's different from Montreal, for sure, but I think I'll enjoy it here." He turned to Maya and smiled. "Especially if I can persuade your sister to spend more time with me."

Smooth. Very smooth. If he kept that up, he wouldn't have much persuading to do. *Watch out, Maya. You're falling hard.*

"I should warn you that my sister is not easily persuaded," Rafe said, as if Maya wasn't sitting right across the table. "You're here, though, so you've already made it further than most guys."

Maya shot him a glare. "Cállate, Rafa."

Colton chuckled. "I've noticed some stubbornness, yes. I'm persistent, though." He reached for another tortilla, and it didn't escape Maya's notice that he filled it with carne asada as opposed to lengua.

"Is that a tattoo on your arm?" Papa asked, frowning for the first time.

Colton glanced down and pulled his sleeve back a little. "Yes."

"Have you been in prison? Or a gang?" Papa demanded.

"Papa!" Maya suddenly wished a hole would open in the floor and swallow her. Mortified, she turned to Colton. "I'm sorry."

He waved a hand. "No need to be." He looked at her father. "No, sir. I'm not in a gang and haven't been in prison." Colton extended his arm so everyone could see the tattoo. "It's a phrase from the French version of the Canadian national anthem," he explained. "Et tu valeur, de foi trempee. It means '*Thy valor steeped in faith.*' It's just my way of honoring my French-Canadian heritage."

The explanation seemed to appease Papa, as he didn't ask any other embarrassing questions, and the rest of the meal passed without tension. Colton ate plenty, which pleased her mother, and tried to explain to Rafe why he believed hockey to be somewhat similar to soccer. Indeed, by the time he polished off a generous slice of tres leches cake for dessert, Colton seemed to have won over her family. As he prepared to leave, Mama invited him back.

"I guess I did okay," Colton said as Maya walked outside with him. "Since I got another invitation."

"Mama likes anyone who brings an appetite," Maya explained. "And you were a very good sport with the lengua."

"It really wasn't too bad," Colton said, and it sounded like he meant it. "It's nice to try something different, and something from your culture. When we're in Montreal, I'll introduce you to poutine."

'We're.' He spoke as if they were a couple. Were they? Had they taken that step? And what did that mean for Maya's job? "What's poutine?" Maya chose the safe question.

"A staple in Quebec." They reached the sidewalk and Colton turned and kept walking. "Trust me, you'll love it."

Maya chuckled softly. "Love it, love it? Or love it in the way you loved the lengua?" she teased. "And by the way, isn't that your car back there?"

"Yes," Colton said. He stopped now that they were past her house. "I'm not taking any chances that anyone's watching from your window. I like your family, but that doesn't mean I want them to see me do this." He lowered his head and brushed his lips across her. The kiss was sweet, tender, different from the explorative one they'd shared before. And oddly, just as passionate.

Now, like before, Maya wanted more, and it was

Colton who pulled away. "Good night, Maya. Thank you for a lovely evening. I'll see you in Montreal."

CHAPTER TEN

Maya took her seat on the commercial airliner, noticing a few of her colleagues from the Generals beat were on the same flight to Montreal, including one she used to work with at the San Antonio Express-News.

"Want to play some cards, Maya?" Joe asked from across the aisle.

"No, thanks. I brought a book. I'm hoping to get some reading done." It was a four hour flight, after all. She'd just pulled the crime thriller from her bag when Shaun barreled his way down the aisle.

"Looks like this is my seat," he said, plopping himself down next to Maya.

Lucky me. "I thought you weren't making the trip to Montreal," she said.

"Change of plans. Found some money in the budget at the last minute," Shaun said. "I don't want to miss this one. The potential for fireworks is too good."

Why was he so convinced that Colton's return to Montreal would be so dramatic? Or was it simply wishful thinking on Shaun's part? If the comments he made were any indication, he definitely liked things on the scandalous side. Maya, on the other hand, hoped only for a Generals victory. And maybe a little time with Colton. "Should be a good game," was all she said before turning her attention to her book.

Fortunately, Shaun didn't bother her for the duration of the flight, instead joining in the card game with some of the reporters. As they landed, though, he turned to Maya. "What do you plan to do before the game? We have a couple hours. Want to take in some sights?"

Maya shook her head. "Not today. I'm just going to head to the hotel and rest a bit, then maybe get to the arena a little early." The lie flowed easily, and apparently convincingly, too, as Shaun didn't question anything, instead simply saying he'd see her in the press box.

Maya did stop by the hotel first, but she didn't stay long. After changing clothes and touching up her makeup, she was out the door again, taking a cab to an address Colton provided her with. It turned out to be a yellow building with orange and blue accenting. She didn't know if the food would be any good at La Banquise, but it was certainly colorful.

She pulled the door open and stepped inside, taking a look around. She almost didn't recognize Colton in sunglasses and a Texas Longhorns baseball cap pulled low on his head, but he gestured her to a small table. "Traveling incognito, I see," Maya said as she sat down.

He gave her a sheepish smile. "Yeah, I figured I better. I don't much care what anyone thinks of me, but I don't want you to get in any trouble."

"That's considerate of you," Maya said. "Why the Longhorns?"

Colton shrugged. "A Generals cap wouldn't be

much of a disguise. I wanted to look like a Texas tourist in Montreal. I figured either this or the Dallas Cowboys would do that, and I remember you saying UT was your alma matter."

It surprised her and flattered her that he would remember. "I almost didn't recognize you, so I think you did well." She looked around. "So what is this place?"

"My favorite place in town to get poutine," Colton said.

"Which is what, exactly?" He still hadn't told her.

"A dish originating here in Quebec. French fries covered with cheese curds and gravy."

"That sounds...interesting." Maya frowned a little.

"You have to try it. C'mon. You made me eat tongue," Colton reminded her.

He had her there. "I'll try it. I just thing it sounds like a strange combination."

"You've had cheese on baked potatoes, right?" Colton challenged. "And gravy on mashed potatoes?"

"Of course."

"So what's strange about cheese and gravy on fried potatoes?"

It was difficult to argue with that logic, so Maya picked up the menu, stunned to see so many different variations on this alleged signature dish. There was poutine with hot dogs, poutine with beef and onions, poutine with butter chicken, even poutine with guacamole. How did one choose?

"I recommend trying the classic poutine," Colton said. "And I usually get La Trois Viandes."

Maya looked at the menu again. That was ground beef, pepperoni and bacon. "The three meats?"

"Very good." Colton grinned. "You'll be speaking French in no time." He waved to a server and then ordered for them in French. Maya noticed he paid the bill right away upon ordering and wondered if that was a local custom.

"I wish we had more time here," he continued. "I'd like to show you more of the city and introduce you to my family."

He wanted her to meet his family. Maya wasn't sure what to think about that, but maybe it shouldn't surprise her. After all, he'd already met hers. "Do you bring a lot of women home to meet your family?" she asked.

Colton frowned and shook his head. "Very few, actually. But I already told you, this is different. *You're* different."

"I want to believe that." *Especially since I might be putting my job on the line by seeing you.*

"Then believe it. I'm not lying to you, Maya. I won't hurt you."

They were bold words coming from a well-known playboy. Could she really trust in their sincerity?

"Ah, here comes our food," Colton said, putting an end to the serious conversation, and sure enough, a heaping plate of french fries, smothered in cheese curds and gravy, was set in front of her.

"That looks like a gastrointestinal attack waiting to happen," Maya observed, nodding at Colton's dish, heaped high with the meat trio atop the standard poutine.

"I have a strong stomach, and I'll burn a lot of calories on the ice tonight." Colton picked up his fork, but instead of using it to dig into his own dish, he pointed at hers. "Okay, try it. Tell me what you think."

Maya used her fork and took a bite. She'd been unsure what to expect, but was pleasantly surprised. It tasted delicious. "I like it," she said, taking another bite.

Colton watched her, a smile on his face. "I figured you would. You've got a little gravy on your lip, though."

"Oh?" She figured he was teasing her. Flirting with her. "Would you like to kiss it away?"

Colton hesitated. "I'm not sure that's a good idea. Someone might see. Montreal's different from San Antonio."

"I'm not afraid, if you're not," Maya challenged. "Besides, who cares if someone sees? We're just a couple of tourists from Texas, after all." He even had the UT cap on to prove it.

"Well, when you put it like that..." Colton leaned over the table and brushed his lips over hers. "Mmm. That gravy tastes so good. And you taste even better."

***

Colton wanted to spend the entire afternoon with Maya, taking her to the Notre Dame Basilica and the Biodome. Instead, duty called and he found himself taking the ice at the Bell Centre for pre-game skate as a member of the visiting team, and finding himself booed.

What the hell? They were booing him in Montreal? His home city, after everything he'd done for the Canadiens franchise, including helping them bring home the Stanley Cup just two seasons ago? Colton hadn't known exactly what to expect in his return to Montreal, but one thing he never expected was to be booed the second he stepped on the ice.

"Ignore it," Trev said, skating up beside him. "Don't let it get to you."

"Easier said than done," Colton muttered.

"I know. I've been there," Trev said. "It's nothing personal, though. You're just the enemy now."

"Yeah." Colton tried to look at it that way. The fans in Montreal were crazy about hockey and their Habs.

While Colton might have achieved great things for the franchise while he played there, he was a General now and the fans' loyalties only lie with the current players on the team. Why should they cheer for a guy who'd been traded?

It was hard not to feel a little nostalgic as a video played in the arena, introducing all of the Habs players, a few of whom Colton still counted as friends. A few, but not all. The crowd was intense, as it always was here, in a rabid hockey city. *No big deal*, he tried to tell himself. In four days, the Generals would have their own season opener, against Columbus, and if the preseason was any indication, they'd have a loud, raucous crowd. Colton looked forward to that, but first it was time to show Montreal what they'd be missing this season.

He lined up in the circle, ready to take the opening face-off against the Habs' Brady McLean. Once teammates, now opponents.

"You ready for this?" McLean asked, and his face seemed to carry a hint of a sneer.

"Ready," Colton said, and touched his stick to the ice. He was ready for the whistle, for the puck drop, for the game.

He won the face off, and McLean dropped his gloves, punching Colton squarely in the jaw.

"I've been waiting for your return, you pansey-assed bastard," McLean said, hitting him again. "Nique ta mere!"

Colton didn't want to fight. He didn't like its place in hockey, but when he heard that, he had little choice to retaliate, and he did so by kneeing Brady McLean in the groin.

Not surprisingly, the ref blew his whistle then, putting an end to the scrum. "Five minutes each for fighting. Number thirty-two Montreal, number nine San Antonio. An additional game misconduct is assessed against San Antonio, number nine, for kneeing," the official said. "The player is ejected from the game."

And just like that, Colton's return to Montreal was over, in the most ignominious way ever.

***

"What was that? What just happened?" Maya watched the opening seconds of the game from the press box, disbelieving. She knew how much Colton looked forward to this game, and she looked forward to watching him play it. Now, suddenly, it was over before it really began, and she was forced to listen to the home-team fans cheer as Colton was escorted off the ice.

"Tremblay got ejected from the game," Shaun said needlessly, and Maya glared at him.

"I know that much." Once he'd kneed the Montreal player, that was a given. "But why did McLean start a fight right with him right away?"And why did Colton risk everything by retaliating? He had to be provoked. That was the only explanation.

"My guess is McLean has some bone to pick with Tremblay," the reporter from the San Antonio newspaper opined.

"Yeah." A Montreal reporter nodded and laughed. "Looks like McLean's still pissed off at Tremblay for fucking his wife."

MICHELE SHRIVER

CHAPTER ELEVEN

Watching the game on the TV monitor in the visitor's locker room after being ejected was not what Colton has in mind for his first game with the Generals. Especially when his new team was getting shellacked on the score board.

At least the team's equipment managers and other assorted personnel gave Colton a wide berth to let him stew and pout on his own. He apologized to his teammates when they came in the room during the first intermission. Down only one to zero at the time, the guys seemed encouraged and no one was too visibly upset with Colton for the situation he'd put them in. It was okay. He'd screwed up, in more ways than one, but the team was hanging tough on the road. It might not win, but as long San Antonio wasn't completely embarrassed, then maybe Colton's moment of infamy wouldn't be the lead-off story on every sportscast in Canada and half the ones in the United States. Maybe.

That hope was short-lived after watching Brady McLean score a hat trick in leading the Canadiens to a seven to one rout. Only a beauty of goal by Nik Brantov, his first in the NHL, saved the Generals from being shut out. Plenty of damage was done, though.

Colton's phone rang as he watched the final minutes of the game, and he knew who it was before he even glanced at the display.

"Rough start for the Generals," his agent said. "Probably would have helped to have their captain and best player on the ice for longer than five seconds."

Great. So Colton was getting the sarcasm treatment. "Spare me the lectures, Scotty. I feel bad enough."

"As you should." Clearly, Scotty wasn't in the mood to cut Colton any slack. "What the hell was that, Tremblay?"

So they weren't even on a first-name basis anymore? Ouch. "Stupidity. I just lost control." As he said it, Colton wondered himself whether he referred to what had happened on the ice, or something else.

"Obviously," the agent replied curtly. "You're better than this, man. Or at least you could be, if you used your brain once in a while."

"I'm sorry, Scott. I let my team down and I let you down," Colton said. "I let everybody down." No one more so than himself.

"You sure as hell did. That was bush league, Tremblay. You'll be lucky if you don't get a call from the player safety and disciplinary committee."

Colton hadn't even thought that far ahead, but the agent was right. He'd almost certainly be fined, or possibly suspended. "Hopefully just a fine," he said, thinking out loud. "I'm not a repeat offender." No, he'd never been an asshole on the ice before. Off it? That was another matter.

"No, and don't become one," Scotty cautioned. "You know, when I said you needed to remake your image, I didn't mean turn into a goon."

"I'm not a goon, and that will never happen again," Colton promised. He watched as the final seconds mercifully ticked off the clock. "Look, I gotta go. The guys will be in the room soon, and I have to figure out what to say. Again, I'm sorry, Scott." The apologies seemed hollow, though, especially when he had to face his teammates, and more importantly, the press.

"Want me to handle the press conference tonight?" The team's oldest veteran, and one of its alternate captains, asked Colton. "Because I can."

Colton appreciated the gesture, but shook his head. "No, man. I need to do it. This one's on me." He just needed to figure out what he would say, especially when it came to Maya. He didn't even want to imagine what she thought of him right now.

***

In some ways, Maya considered it a blessing that the hockey game was a complete disaster for the Generals, because she didn't pay close enough attention to it to accurately and intelligently report on it. No, she'd been far too busy investigating the Montreal reporter's claim that Colton slept with his former teammate's wife.

She couldn't find any hard, concrete evidence— was she expecting a sex tape? —but the internet was full of rumors, gossip and innuendo about Colton and Jana McLean, including speculation by one media outlet that it was, in fact, Brady McLean that pressured the Canadiens organization to trade one of its best players in an effort to save his marriage. With Colton out of Montreal, Brady apparently thought Jana would be less likely to stray. But even after getting his wish with the trade, it seemed Brady still harbored some animosity toward his former teammate, at least judging from his decision to slug Colton seconds after the game began.

Professional, Maya. Keep it professional, she cautioned herself as she waited with the horde of other reporters to be allowed access to the locker room for the post-game press briefing. Would that even be possible, though, when just a few hours before the game she'd been sharing poutine and kisses with the team captain? Did that qualify as professional? Not hardly. It all served as another reminder of why it was such a bad idea to allow herself to get personally involved with Colton. It was too late for that, though. She'd officially fallen, and fallen hard.

And for what? To find out that he had so little respect for marriage and commitment that he'd sleep with a married woman, to say nothing of the fact that team loyalty didn't seem to matter much, either. No. If the rumors about Colton and Jana McLean were true—and there seemed to be an awful of smoke, even if she hadn't seen the fire—then Maya needed to cut her losses.

She stifled a gasp when saw the cut on Colton's face and the bruises already forming around his eye. He'd have a heck of a shiner, for sure. Maya had to give him credit, though, as he stepped forward to take their questions. There'd been plenty of speculation in the booth that Colton would not make himself available to the press, instead letting one of the team's alternate captains handle the media.

"Before I take questions, there's something I want to say," Colton began. "I've already apologized to my teammates for my actions tonight, but I owe an apology to our fans, too. What they saw tonight, in the brief time I was on the ice, was not the player I am. I look forward to the next game to show them that."

"What do you mean when you say that's not the player you are? Are you saying you're not someone who knees opposing players in the groin, or you're not someone who sleeps with your teammate's wife?" Shaun Stanton demanded. "Or both?"

This time, Maya did gasp. She hadn't expected anyone to give Colton a break, and he probably didn't deserve one. Still, it took incredible gall for Shaun to ask such a question point blank, even if it was one all of them wanted to ask.

Colton must have expected the question, because he didn't even flinch. "I'm going to limit my responses to the game," he said. "I'm a player who prides himself on always giving everything to his team, and I didn't do that tonight."

Shaun guffawed. "No, but I hear you gave plenty of yourself to Jana McLean, and it looks like Brady boy is still pissed about it."

"That's enough!" The team's alternate captain, Alex Gray, stepped forward. "If any of you actually have questions about the game we just played, I'll answer those now."

***

Colton intended to face the vultures like a man, but he was relieved when Alex took over. At least he could keep things slightly focused on the game, not that there had been much good to say about it. He had to hand it to Alex, though. The long-time NHL vet managed to keep things on a positive note, talking about things they could build on for the next game. *Yeah, and maybe they'll even have their captain.* At least if Colton wasn't suspended by the league.

He noticed Maya was quiet during the whole thing, not asking a single question. As soon as Alex held up a hand signaling he was done taking questions and the reporters were ushered out of the locker room, Colton went after them. He didn't care what anyone else thought right now. He needed to see Maya. Talk to her. Try to explain.

Instead, he got out in the hallway and found her already gone. Instead, the jackass who'd tried to ask Colton about Jana was still there. Of course he was. Some guys never quit. Well, if he thought he could get an exclusive scoop, he was sorely mistaken.

Colton brushed past the guy, heading for the exit door. If there was one advantage of being ejected from the game, it was that he was already out of uniform and dressed in street clothes. He wasn't fast enough, though. When he got out of the arena, there was no sign of Maya.

The bunnies, however, were there and waiting, including one Colton recognized. The woman he'd spent the night with the day before he learned he'd been traded. It now seemed like a lifetime ago.

"There you are, Colton," she purred. What the hell was her name? Ariel? No. Arianne. That was it. "You never called me back."

"No, I didn't. Sorry about that."

"That's okay, baby. You can make it up to me tonight."

CHAPTER TWELVE

Maya felt like a coward, hurrying out of the arena and back to the hotel. As if avoiding Colton forever were really an option. He knew exactly where to find her, and her job—for as long as she still had it—put them in close proximity. Besides, who was she fooling? She didn't really want to avoid him. She wanted to spend as much time as possible with him. She just wanted to believe he was the man he claimed to be, not the one that Montreal gossip rags made him out to be.

"So which is it, Colton? Who's the real you?" she asked as she hastily packed the suitcase she'd just unpacked that afternoon, when she'd arrived in Montreal. The truth, she figured, lay somewhere in between. That's what her brother, the cop, often said. Maya realized she could probably live with that, as long as the truth fell closer to one side than the other. She wouldn't know, though, unless she gave him a chance to explain and she couldn't do that by running.

"Don't be stupid," she chastised herself, and stopped packing. It was nothing more than a silly distraction. It was now eleven p.m. The possibility of getting a flight that night was slim to none, and besides, even if she left, Colton would still catch up to her in Ottawa the next day. Not only would running away not solving anything, it wasn't possible.

Her phone rang, and Maya reached for it, expecting it might be Colton. Instead, it was Shaun.

"Want to grab a late dinner or a drink downstairs?" he asked. "It turns out I'm just a few doors down from you."

Great. It seemed Maya couldn't avoid him, as much as she might want to. "Not tonight. I still have some work to finish up," she said. "And I do want to get some sleep." She hoped he'd get the message and wouldn't persist further. Surely by this point he ought to be getting the clue that she wasn't interested. Maya held her breath.

Shaun let out a sigh. "Fine. Suit yourself," he said. "But I'll be downstairs if you change your mind about that drink after you finish your work."

"I'll keep that in mind," Maya lied. "Thanks."

The excuse she'd given Shaun was basically true. Her story was finished, but would still need updating if more news filtered in. And she really did want to get some decent sleep before the early morning flight to Ottawa. Maya turned her phone off and went to get ready for bed.

***

Arianne was nothing if not bold and aggressive, and she didn't wait for Colton to respond before going in for the kiss. The cheap perfume she wore was familiar, and Colton still had vivid memories of the things she could do for him. So vivid, in fact, that his groin tightened instinctively.

"What do you say? One more time, Colt?" The words came out in a breathy whisper as Ariane's hand found his crotch, causing him to stiffen even more.

Jesus. Colton sucked in a breath. So far, Arianne was the only person in the world who'd ever called him 'Colt' and he knew the moniker was in reference to his sexual prowess. It was tempting, very tempting, especially given the increasing tightness down below. But that was the reason he was in the mess in the first place. If he'd been able to keep his dick in his pants when he'd played here, Colton would probably still be a member of the Montreal Canadiens, and he most certainly wouldn't be sporting one hell of a black eye courtesy of a former teammate.

His mind flashed to his agent's warning, the words of advice from Trevor Collison, and to Maya. Most importantly to Maya. Colton had told her things were different, he was different now. All because she was so vastly different than any woman he'd met before. He wanted to know her better. He wanted to be with Maya, not Arianne or any of the other women standing outside the arena who had no self-respect. How could they, if their only goal in life was to score with an NHL player who'd forget all about them by morning?

"No thanks, Arianne." Colton pulled away from her clawing hands. "There's someone else I need to see." *Assuming she still wants anything to do with me.* That was doubtful, at least if Maya knew why Brady McLean had a bone to pick with Colton. Still, he had to try.

The late night air was brisk for October, even in Canada, and Colton pulled his sport coat closed and buttoned it. The hotel was only two blocks from the arena, and he figured the walk would do him good. It wasn't like he got any exercise playing in the game.

Colton tried to call Maya, but she either wasn't answering or her phone was off. He preferred to think the latter, not wanting to acknowledge that maybe she'd chosen to ignore him. Fine. He'd stop by her room, instead. She'd have a harder time ignoring him if he showed up in person.

He knocked on the door and waited. After what seemed like and eternity, he heard Maya's muffled voice through the door. "Colton?"

She must have looked through the peep hole. "Yes, it's me, Maya. Can I come in?"

The door opened, and Maya stood there, dressed only in a dark green nightgown that didn't waste much fabric, which looked to be silk, and highlighted every single one of her sensuous curves. Sweet, holy hell she was beautiful, and this time as Colton's cock stirred, Arianne was a distant memory. There was only one woman he wanted, and she was right in front of him, her expression wary. "I was just about to go to bed," Maya said.

As much as he wanted to join her there, and not for sleep, Colton bit back any remarks of that nature, knowing they wouldn't be appreciated. Especially not now. "I'd like to talk to you," he said. "Explain what happened at the game, and why." He'd been curt with the press when they'd tried to ask him about Jana, and Maya was the press, but Colton wanted her to know the truth, even if he wasn't very proud of it. "Can I come in?"

***

Maya hesitated. The smart response would be to say no. She shouldn't let him in; shouldn't let things go any further that they already had. Except it had already gone too far to turn back. "It's late. I'm tired," she said, but stepped aside to let him in.

Colton nodded. "Then I won't stay very long." He stepped into the room and Maya closed the door. "I just don't want to leave things the way they are, when you're probably thinking the worst about me."

His hands were jammed in his pockets and his eyes downcast, giving Colton a vulnerable look. How was it that Maya saw him so differently than the rest of her colleagues? Was he different around her, or was she simply gullible and stupid? "I admittedly haven't seen you play very often, but that definitely wasn't your finest moment in a game." Maya also knew he hadn't started the fight, and the bruising around his eye appeared to be getting worse. "Can I get you some ice for your face?"

"What, this?" Colton brought his hand to eye, then shook his head. "Nah. I'll be fine. Physically, anyway." He let out a sigh. "I'll probably get fined for kneeing McLean in the nuts."

"I heard that, yes," Maya said.

"Not exactly the best way to reform my image. My agent's pretty pissed."

"So why'd you do it? You've never had a reputation for fighting before." Other things, yes. But not that.

"You speak Spanish. What's the worst thing you can say to someone? You know, to really insult or offend them?"

Now he wanted to know about Spanish swear words? Maya hesitated. "I don't like to say it, but... *chinga tu madre*." She swallowed hard. "It literally means 'fuck your mother.'" Maya hoped she'd be forgiven for talking that way. "You should never say that to a Mexican."

"Just like you should never to a say to a Frenchman *nique ta mere*." Colton appeared to almost spit the words. "I may get fined, but I couldn't let McLean get away with that."

"So you kneed McLean in the groin because he insulted your mother," Maya surmised, her lips turning up in a slight smile. That, at least, was something she could respect. "It doesn't explain why he would choose to attack you like that, or give you that black eye. I do know a little bit about hockey, and I know games don't usually start with fights off of the opening face off."

"They don't, you're right," Colton said. "I deserve the shiner, and maybe a lot more. McLean has a reason for hating me." He looked her in the eye. "Come on, you're a good reporter. I think you have a pretty solid idea what that reason is."

"It's true, then. You had an affair with his wife."

"Yes."

Maya wanted the real truth from him, but she never expected it to be so easily forthcoming. He'd clammed up in the press briefing, deflected their questions, and let a teammate come to his rescue. Only to come to her room and admit it so freely. "Why?"

"Why?" Colton repeated, and only then did Maya realize she'd spoken the word out loud.

"Never mind. I don't need to know why."

"I'll tell you anyway. Because Brady's an ass, and Jana's hot. Crazy hot, but there's something sweet about her too. And they were separated at the time. She told me they were done. She planned to divorce him. She said she wanted to be with me, and I wanted to believe it. More than anything in the world, I wanted to believe it. Not that any of that matters. I tried to tell myself it did, to somehow absolve myself of guilt or wrongdoing, but the truth is, I'm an ass too. You'd be wise not have anything more to do with me." Colton started for the door. "I'll go now. I just wanted you to know the truth."

"What?" Maya couldn't believe what she'd just heard. Oh, not the confession. She'd known the truth before he'd admitted it, though it was a different truth that she'd imagined. Had Colton fallen in love with Jana, only to have her change her mind about her marriage and walk away from him? "You're just going to leave? That's it? I'm an ass. You shouldn't get involved with me. And see ya?"

Colton turned back around to face her. "Isn't that what you want? I walk away and go back to doing what I do best. Play hockey. And you report on it. We forget Paloma Blanca, William Barret Travis and the fudge at the Alamo. Lengua, poutine... none of that ever happened. You do your job, I do mine. Other than that, we don't see each other. Strictly professional. That's what you want, right?"

He was partially right. It was what her brain insisted she wanted, but her heart and everything other aspect of her body begged to differ. "What do *you* want, Colton?"

"Oh, that's easy. The same thing I've wanted since the very first day I was traded to the Generals and I saw you on the video conference and you asked me about the trade. I want to be the best player in the NHL, and I want to be thought of as a good guy. A good captain. A good teammate. Not the jackass I was when I played here." He took a deep breath and looked her right in the eye. "More than that, though, I want you, Maya Dominguez. I want you and me. I want 'us.' That's what *I* want. Can you say the same?"

This time, her heart won the struggle over her head. "Yes, Colton," Maya said. "It's what I want too."

CHAPTER THIRTEEN

They were the words Colton wanted to hear, but could he trust that he'd heard them right? "You mean that? You want me? You want us?"

"Yes," Maya said without hesitation. "If I'm to be perfectly honest, it's what I've wanted for a long time. I just... held back, tried to convince myself otherwise. Because of my job."

Her job, yes. There was that to consider, but Colton knew it was more. "Not just your job. Because of me, right? My past. My history."

"That too," Maya admitted. "I wasn't sure I could trust you, and I wanted more than to be just another groupie, or another woman you used and discarded, like Jana McLean."

"No." Colton shook his head vehemently. "It wasn't like that with Jana. I didn't use Jana. No, if anything, she used me." Now that it was over, with time and distance between them, Colton could look back on it with less anger, at least toward Jana. Brady, on the other hand, was another matter. "That's beside the point, though. It doesn't matter. What matters now is us." He reached out and took her hand. "I've told you before, this is no game, Maya. This time, I'm playing for keeps."

"You've said that, yes." Her lips curled in a smile. "And you even ate tongue to try to prove it. And put up with my crazy family."

"That's right. So have I proven myself to you?" Colton asked. "Or is there anything else I need to do?"

Maya appeared to think for a minute. "Actually, there is something else..."

Colton bit his bottom lip. He'd do it, no questions asked, but she was one stubborn woman. "Name it, anything."

"Make love to me," Maya said. "And I don't just mean sex."

"Oh, honey, I already know that with you, it will never be 'just sex.'" As Colton pulled her into his arms, he realized that exactly why he wanted her so much. "And I very much welcome the opportunity to prove it to you," he added, kissing her.

***

Colton's lips met hers, and gone was the uncertain exploration of their first kiss, or the sweet, tenderness of the second. This one was hungry, searching, wanting, and Maya welcomed it.

"You shouldn't have opened the door dressed like that," Colton whispered as he nuzzled on her lower lip, then her neck. "You can drive a man wild."

"I told you, I was getting ready for bed..."

"And that's exactly where we're going, but I hope you don't expect to get much sleep."

A soft chuckle escaped from Maya's throat, but she knew he wasn't joking. Everything from the desire in his eyes to the movements of his hands and his hardness pressing against her told Maya that slumber wasn't on the agenda. And that suited her just fine.

"Sleep is overrated," Maya said, and pulled her

nightgown over her head so she stood before him, wearing only a leopard-print thong.

"Vous êtes si belle, ma chérie." Colton's voice was barely a whisper.

"What does that mean?" Maya asked. She'd definitely have to learn some French if this continued. *If?* Who was she fooling? Things had already gone too far to walk away.

"You are so beautiful, my darling," Colton translated, his gaze holding hers. "I'm going to have to teach you French," he said. "But first, I want to touch and kiss every inch of your body."

The mere words made Maya tremble with pleasure, and she was glad when Colton gently laid her down on the bed. At least that way if she went weak under his touch, she wouldn't faint to the floor. *No fainting allowed, Maya.* No, she wanted to be conscious and alert for every minute of this. "Every inch?" she challenged in a teasing voice. "Can you really do that?"

Colton smiled down at her. "I sure intend to try."

And try he did, first caressing and kissing her face, then her neck. He even gave her shoulder blades attention before moving to her breasts, taking one in his hand while his mouth devoured the other. Maya let out a moan as Colton nibbled her nipple. So far, so good. She'd have to remember to challenge him more often.

Pleasure coursed through her as Colton's hands continued their journey, finally reaching inside her underwear to find her wet center. "Oh God," Maya cried out as his finger thrust inside her. "Colton!"

"Just Colton is fine." He grinned and inserted another finger, moving them against her core with increasing pressure until finally Maya couldn't stand it any further and she cried out, her body convulsing with pleasure.

"That's it, stay like that," Colton said as his free hand fumbled with his pants. "Touch yourself if you have to, but wait for me, ma cherie."

Touch herself? Maya tried not to think about what the sisters at her Catholic elementary school would think, or how Colton sheathed himself with a condom with the quick, expert movements of one who had done so many times, and simply did as he asked, touching her fingers to her sensitive bud.

The friction has the desired effect, and instead of diminishing, Maya's pleasure grew, finally reaching a crescendo as Colton thrust himself inside her, where they moved together until they went over the brink at the same time.

***

Colton was fairly certain he'd made good on his promise to kiss every inch of Maya's delectable body the night before, but just in case there was any doubt, he decided to wake her up by planting a trail of kisses up her leg.

"Mmm. This is nice," she murmured. "A girl could get used this."

"Go ahead and get used to it," Colton whispered between kisses. "If you stay with me, it'll be happening a lot." There were a few things in life Colton knew with certainty. He was good at hockey. He was good at pleasuring women. And he wanted to spend a lot more time with Maya, in and out of the bedroom.

He was rock hard, but in no hurry to enter her, instead taking his time, wanting her to drive her to the brink and leave her begging for him. What Colton was unprepared for was the screech of an alarm clock interrupting their foreplay. It startled him to the point that he damn near jumped. "Bon sang!"

Maya bolted up. "I have to get ready. I have to get to the airport!"

"Right now?" Colton couldn't keep the disappointment from his voice. A quick glance at the bedside clock confirmed that while he had a little time to spare, it wasn't much. He'd have to leave pretty soon too, if he didn't want to be a late to a team meeting.

"I can spare a few minutes. Can you hurry?"

Could he hurry? Colton stifled a chuckle. "It's been a long time since I've gotten that request." He aimed to please, though, and quickly sheathed himself before slipping inside her.

Their coupling was more frantic than Colton would have liked, and he was fairly certain Maya felt the same way, but it was satisfying nonetheless. Still, it made Colton long for a day off and to be back home together so they could enjoy each other without interruptions.

Home. As Maya slipped out of the bed to go to the shower, Colton was struck by how quickly he'd come to consider San Antonio home. And he knew the reason why.

"You can let yourself out?" Maya asked.

"Yeah. I need to get going myself so I can meet up with the team."

"I'll see you in Ottawa," she said. "Then we'll be home."

Yeah. When Colton would have to face the hometown fans after failing his team in the season opener. He was ready, though. With Maya by his side, he felt as if he could conquer anything. "I can't wait," he said, then gave her a kiss before she headed to the shower.

***

107

He was gone by the time Maya emerged from the bathroom, which at least ensured they wouldn't get distracted and she wouldn't miss her flight. Too bad. She wouldn't mind getting carried away with Colton again.

Instead, reality awaited. It was time to get back to work, on to game two in Ottawa. Already, Maya felt out of touch and a step behind after spending the entire night disconnected from her computer and social media. Although she could imagine what the stories would be saying about Colton and his return to Montreal, Maya didn't know for sure. She'd filed her report as soon as the game ended, updated it once with a few quotes from the press conference after the game, then spent the evening in sexual bliss with the team captain. Everything about the night was great, but what now? He was a hockey player, and she was a beat reporter.

Check that. She was a beat reporter who had six text messages from her boss.

What's up? Frank wanted to know. *Your story's not updated and you're not tweeting.*

Busted! *Sorry,* Maya typed back. *Internet's been sketchy here. Headed to the airport. Will work before the flight.*

Liar. She was such a liar, blaming the Wi-fi in Canada for not being able to do her job. But what could she say? Sorry, Frank, I was too busy screwing Colton Tremblay's brains out? No. That wouldn't do.

Fortunately, Frank didn't press the issue, simply replying that he'd see her when she got back. With her boss temporarily placated, Maya shoved her phone into her handbag and gathered her things to leave. As she opened the door of her room, she found Shaun standing in the hallway.

"Morning." He greeted her with a smile. "Are you heading to the airport?"

Why did she get the impression he'd been waiting outside her door? "Yes."

"Great. We can share a cab."

Maya didn't want to, but it wasn't something she could really say no to. After all, they were leaving at the same time and going to the same place. "Fine," she said, but without enthusiasm.

"So did you have a good night?" Shaun asked as they fell into step together on the way to the elevator. "Get a lot of rest?"

"Yes." *Not at all.* "What did you do?"

"Oh, nothing too exciting. Finished up some new stories for the blog." Shaun pressed the button for the elevator. "You should check them out."

MICHELE SHRIVER

CHAPTER FOURTEEN

Infamy in Montreal. Next stop, Ottawa. It was anyone's guess why the league made the Generals start the season with two road games, back to back, in Canada. Award an expansion team, then punish it with a brutal schedule. Colton was anxious to get back to San Antinio, step on home ice, and start making things right with the fans there. Instead, he was headed to Ottawa. The saving grace was that another game right away meant a chance to erase last night's ugly memories from people's minds.

He returned to the team hotel just in time for a team meeting before boarding their charter plane to the Canadian capital. Although Colton hadn't skipped out on any team activities or meetings the night before, he expected there might still be a few questions as to why he'd been absent from the team's hotel overnight and returned wearing the same clothes from the night before. Sure enough, Coach Moreau was waiting for him.

"Nice of you to show up, Tremblay."

"I wouldn't miss a meeting or the plane," Colton said, feeling contrite. As amazing as the night with Maya had been, it wasn't in the greatest judgment. After vowing to turn over a new leaf, Colton still couldn't seem to stop letting his teammates down.

"I didn't think you would," the coach said, "but you were starting to have me a little worried. I made you the captain because I thought you had the potential to be a good leader, on and off the ice. I've seen some things over the past month that support that, but unfortunately, I've also seen some things that make me worry you're still the same immature punk that your hometown team couldn't wait to be rid of."

Colton swallowed hard as his coach's blunt words sunk in. He didn't expect coddling, but the truth really hurt.

"I don't want it to be a mystery whether Good Colton or Bad Colton shows up on any given day," the other man continued. "We need Good Colton. No exceptions."

Colton nodded, meeting his coach's discerning gray eyes. "I understand that, sir. I know I let a lot of people down in last night's game."

"You sure did." No, he definitely wasn't being cut any slack. "I'm concerned about what happened in the game, don't get me wrong," Coach said. "But I'm also very concerned about what apparently happened before the game and after it."

"I'm not sure what you mean." Colton chose his words carefully.

"Then I guess you haven't seen this. You were probably too busy sneaking out of a certain reporter's hotel room." Moreau handed Colton a piece of paper. It wasn't a newspaper, but rather a printout from a website. A popular sports gossip website. Colton froze as he looked at the article.

Can leopards change their spots?

*San Antonio Generals captain Colton Tremblay promised
he was a changed man after unceremoniously being dumped by his
hometown team and being sent to hockey exile in central Texas.
Instead, as his return to Montreal showed, Tremblay is still up to
his old tricks.*

*The team's charter had barely landed at the Montreal
airport when Tremblay was spotted in a lip lock at a popular local
eatery. The stunning brunette Tremblay chose to play tonsil hockey
with looks suspiciously like a member of the press corps in town to
cover the game. Although Tremblay tried for a disguise, it wasn't a
very good one.*

Colton felt slightly sick to his stomach as he
looked at the picture. No, his disguise wasn't very good.
It was clearly him, kissing Maya, a heaping helping of
poutine on the table between them. Although he didn't
want to, Colton read on.

*Hey, it's a good thing Tremblay got a little hockey in
yesterday, since we all know how the game turned out. Twenty
PIMs in four seconds of ice time? That might be a record. In
fairness, the melee was initiated by Brady McLean, giving credence
to the rumors that the Canadiens winger might have been responsible
for forcing Tremblay out of town.*

*Although the Generals captain tried to appear contrite in
the post-game briefing, one wonders how much he's really learned,
since he was spotted leaving the hotel room of the same reporter in
the wee hours of the morning, after apparently spending the night.
One can only imagine what went on in there. Perhaps Tremblay was
simply trying to score some much-needed favorable press. Wink
wink.*

He sure won't be getting it from this reporter.

Colton glanced at the reporter's byline. Shaun
Stanton. He should've guessed. The guy always seemed
out to get Colton from the very day he'd gotten his press
creds. And instead of being wary and cautious, Colton fell

right into Stanton's trap.

Son of a bitch. He passed the paper back to his coach. "It's not quite as bad as it looks."

"Really?" Moreau raised a bushy eyebrow. "That's interesting, because it looks pretty damn bad. I want an explanation, Tremblay. And you owe your team one too."

Colton knew that, and he'd have to figure out what to say pretty quickly. At the moment, though, he was more worried about Maya.

***

Her phone rang a few minutes before Maya was due to board her flight to Ottawa to rejoin the team for the second game. It was Frank.

"What? I have to board in a few minutes."

"Change of plans," Frank said. "You're not going to Ottawa to cover the Generals game against the Senators. I'm sending Smith. He's already on his way to the airport."

"What the hell?" Maya demanded. "Why, Frank? I told you why I was a little out of touch last night. My story has been updated, though, and I'll get a better Wi-fi card for these international trips."

"Yeah, I just saw the updates," Frank said. "Good job pulling in quotes from the Montreal players."

Maya had just finished the story from the airport terminal, and she'd had to rely on one of her Montreal counterparts to include the quotes—all of which were about the game, not McLean versus Tremblay—but she got it done. "So why are you pulling me off?"

"Because you lied to me. I don't think you were 'out of touch' because of internet issues. I think you were distracted last night."

There was something about the way he said 'distracted' that Maya didn't like. Then again, she didn't like anything about the conversation so far. "What are you talking about?"

Frank let out an audible sigh. "Apparently you haven't seen Sports Chatter's hockey page this morning."

"No, I've been busy updating my story, not reading other people's." As she said, it, though, she opened her web browser and entered the URL. The page loaded quickly—a reminder that her Wi-fi card was perfectly fine—and Maya was greeted with a picture of herself. Kissing Colton.

As a mixture of dread and panic came over her, Maya skimmed the article. It was all about Colton and never mentioned her by name, but the picture was damning to anyone who knew Maya's face. Her boss obviously did. "I can explain, Frank," she said. At the moment, though, she had no idea how.

"Great! I look forward to hearing that explanation. You can give it to me in person when you get back to San Antonio. I strongly urge you to get on the next available flight." There was a click and the line went dead. He'd hung up, without telling Maya if she still had a job.

If she did, and wanted to keep it, Maya knew she better find a flight back to Texas, and fast. But there was one thing she needed to do first. She marched over to where Shaun sat, waiting to board the flight to Ottawa that she now wouldn't be on.

"You son of a bitch!"

He glanced up at her with an amused smirk. "I guess you finally deigned yourself to stoop low enough to read my work."

"Stoop low is right! You said you wrote a hockey blog."

"It *is* a hockey blog."

"Really?" Maya scoffed. "Because what I just looked at reads a lot more like TMZ than SB Nation."

"Just reporting the team news. Sorry you had to get caught in the crossfire." Shaun's tone carried no hint of regret.

The gate agent announced the pre-boarding of the flight and Shaun stood up. "Looks like I have to get on a plane. Are you coming, Maya?"

She glared at him. "Not to Ottawa, no. I have to back to San Antonio. Thanks to you."

"Too bad." Shaun shrugged. "No hard feelings, I hope. I mean, I'm sure things will work out fine for you. Big shot reporter that you are. The cream always rises to the top and all that." He smirked. "Isn't that what you told me when you got the sports editor position at The Daily Texan?"

"So that's what this is about? You're still upset that I beat you out for the job you wanted with the student newspaper?" Maya knew Shaun had a jealous streak, but it seemed a little ridiculous to still hold a grudge about something that happened in college.

"Yeah, because you landed a great job straight out of J-school and never had to pay your dues. Unlike me."

Maya bristled. "I've paid dues. I've paid dues every day, being a woman and Hispanic. But you're right. The cream rises. I'll be just fine, because I'm a good reporter. You, on the other hand, will never amount to more than a glorified gossip columnist." She turned to walk away.

"That's it? That's your best comeback?" Shaun laughed. "Have a good flight back to Texas, Maya."

***

Colton owned up to poor judgment and letting his team down, and vowed to bring his A-game to their matchup with the Ottawa Senators. The guys all said they had his back and were on his side, and all the other things they were expected to say. Talk was cheap, though. Colton knew he had to deliver on the ice, or it wouldn't take long for the guys to turn on him.

He didn't want that to happen, so Colton gave everything to their practice skate at the Senators' arena. He led the team through the crease challenge and was the first on the team to complete the stop and start. By the time practice was over and it was time to face the press, Colton was exhausted but anxious for the game to start.

"Great practice out there today. The ice seems to be in good shape and we're excited about tonight," he said, opening the press briefing. Colton scanned the room, but Maya wasn't there. What the hell was going on?

"You seemed to be pushing yourself pretty hard out there today," a reporter from TSN said. "Do you think you'll have enough left in the tank for the game."

"Absolutely," Colton said without hesitation, then cracked a slight smile. "It's not like I played much last night."

A few chuckles sounded throughout the room, relaxing Colton a little. He ignored the asshole who'd penned the column for Sports Chatter and turned his attention to a reporter he didn't know.

"Brad Smith, All Sports Today San Antonio," the guy said, and Colton didn't hear the question that followed. He had one of his own.

"Where's Maya?"

"Oh, she's not on this beat anymore."

MICHELE SHRIVER

CHAPTER FIFTEEN

Instead of a quick flight to Ottawa and being there for the Generals press briefing after the morning skate, Maya flew from Montreal to New York City to Dallas and finally back to San Antonio. She tried to call Frank again, but he was curt, simply telling her he'd see her when she got back to town. It was late afternoon when she finally did, exhausted from a long day of travel and being in four airports. She went straight to the news bureau, anxious to find out whether she still had a job. If the news was bad, maybe it was best to just get it over with.

Frank waited for her, but fortunately everyone else was either gone for the day or on assignment somewhere. Maya didn't want an audience when she was chewed out.

"How was the flight?" Frank asked.

"You mean all three of them?" Maya set her computer case on her desk and sat down. "Long, but I'm here." Ready to face the music.

Frank nodded and rolled his chair closer. "I sent

Brad to cover the game in Ottawa."

Maya nodded. She expected Brad would get the assignment. The question was did he now have it permanently? "He'll do a good job," she said. "Just like I would have done a good job."

"Would you have?" Frank arched an eyebrow above his wire-rimmed glasses. "Or would you to be too distracted by watching your boyfriend to really pay attention to the game?"

"Low blow, Frank." Except Maya knew she deserved it.

"You said you had an explanation for the article on the Chatter site. Let's hear it."

Maya took a breath. "The guy that wrote the article, Shaun Stanton, is someone I went to school with. We dated for a while, nothing too serious. I was more focused on my studies." Idly, she wondered if Shuan's apparent grudge against her was professional jealousy, or personal because she wasn't really interested in a relationship with him. "We competed for the same internships, things like that. In our last year, I got the sports editor position with the UT newspaper. The position that Shaun really coveted."

"So you're saying this guy is jealous of your success and out to get you in trouble?" Frank rubbed his goatee.

"The thought crossed my mind." And Shaun hadn't done much to dispel it when she confronted him at the airport.

"And that wasn't really you kissing Trembaly? This Stanton guy photoshopped you in the picture? And Tremblay wasn't sneaking out of your hotel room this morning?" Frank's tone made it clear he didn't believe that for a second.

"I didn't say that." Maya averted a gaze, instead concentrating on the blotter on her desk.

Her boss sighed. "You said you had this under control, Maya; that you weren't in over your head."

"At the time I wasn't." Maya knew it wasn't entirely true. The line was already dangerously close to being crossed when she'd accompanied Colton to dinner his first night in town. "Things just got a little out of control. I'm sorry, Frank. I know it's unprofessional."

"It sure as hell is, which is why I had to pull you off the beat immediately," he said. "I can't jeopardize this organization's credibility any more than it already is."

Maya nodded. She understood it wasn't personal. Frank was simply doing what he had to. "So I'm off the Generals beat. Am I out of a job too? Should I start clearing out my desk?"

"I don't want to lose you, Maya. In spite of this, you're a damn good reporter." Frank let out a sigh. "We need someone regular to cover the high schools again. Bouncing it around among three different people isn't working."

High school. From the National Hockey League back to the local high schools. It was hard to sink much lower than that. "That far, Frank? You can't even trust me with UTSA's sports teams?"

"Not right now. There is an alternative, though. A way you can keep the Generals beat."

"How?" Maya was skeptical.

"Tremblay has a reputation as a player. Everyone knows that. The article this morning was really about his actions, the fact he hasn't changed at all," Frank said. "It even comes out and accuses him of trying to win favor with the press corps. I think we can spin that in our favor. If you're on board."

He didn't say it out loud, but Maya knew what Frank was suggesting, and it made her a little sick. "In other words, I throw Colton under the bus and never have anything to do with him again. I do that, and I can keep the Generals beat?"

"That's right." Frank looked at his watch. "The game's about to start, and I know you're tired. Why don't you go watch the game, think about what it would be like watching it from the press box, and give me an answer tomorrow."

***

Colton led the team onto the ice at the Canadian Tire Centre. Game two in as many nights, but for him, it would essentially be only one. After this, they'd head back to San Antonio and get ready for their home opener against Columbus in two nights. There was a big difference between being one and one and being zero and two. Colton was determined to do everything he could to make it one and one. To do that, though, he'd have to focus.

He'd tried to reach Maya several times during the afternoon, but to no avail. Colton knew she was probably on a flight back to San Antonio, but he didn't know for sure why. All he knew was the last time they'd spoken, she said she'd see him in Ottawa. Instead, that Smith guy showed up instead of her. Had she been pulled off the hockey beat because of the article in Sports Chatter, or worse yet, had she been fired because of it? Or was her absence not because of the article, but because of Colton? Had she simply chosen to walk away from him, and what they could be together?

The latter scenario was what worried Colton the most. He didn't want to go through anything like that again. Being jilted once was enough, and this time would be worse. Colton had cared deeply for Jana, even thought he could love her, but he realized now his feelings for Jana would never compare to his feelings for Maya.

"Look for rebounds." The directive came from Trev, and redirected Colton's focus to where it needed to be. The game.

"What do you mean?"

"I used to play here, remember? I know King's strengths and I know his weaknesses," Trev said, referring to the Senators goaltender. He smiled. "He has a tendency to give up some sloppy rebounds sometimes."

"Got it," Colton said. "Thanks for the tip."

This time, there was no fight off the opening face-off. The Ottawa player won it, and the game began uneventfully, which Colton was immensely relieved about. No one hated him here. No one booed him. He didn't have anything to prove to the Senators fans.

Trev did, however. Three minutes into the game, he took a pass from Nik and fired it on net. The Ottawa goalie made the save but couldn't control the rebound. The puck spun loose and Colton was there, aiming top shelf above King's shoulder.

One-zero Generals.

As Colton toward the bench for the celebratory fist-bump with his teammates, his thoughts drifted again to Maya.

Was she watching the game? Had she seen the goal? Did she even care?

***

Since she wasn't ready to go home to her parents' house and explain why she was back from Canada a day early and not working the hockey game, Maya went to a popular downtown sports bar to watch it on TV. She took a seat the bar and ordered a locally-brewed beer and an order of French fries. Was it weird that she almost asked if she could get cheese curds and gravy on the fries?

Maya took a swallow of beer and listened to chatter from the patrons around her as they waited for the game to start. A few fans seemed antsy and angry about the night before. Tremblay better produce tonight, or else, Maya heard one guy proclaim. Or else what? Shouldn't Colton get more than one game before the local fans turned on him? It apparently depended on who you asked, because another guy jumped to his defense.

The chatter was completely different from the kind that went on in the press box prior to the game, but it was interesting to listen to. Maya couldn't escape the irony that she'd tried to turn into a hockey fan in order to be better at her job, and here she was, suddenly forced to watch the game as a 'fan.'

She watched nervously as Colton lined up for the opening face-off and exhaled when there was no fight to start the game. Maybe this would just be about hockey and not personal grudges. For Colton's sake, Maya hoped so. Three minutes in, he scored, giving San Antonio the lead and Maya cheered as loud as everyone else in the bar.

"See, I said we had to give him a chance," the bar patron who'd defended Colton said to his friend.

"More of that, and I will," the other guy said.

A woman at the bar had an opinion too. "Tremblay's so freaking hot," she announced.

"Too bad he knows it," another said, and this time Maya wanted to jump to his defense.

None of these people knew him. They didn't know him at all. But did Maya know him any better? Did she know him well enough to give up her dream job for him? It wasn't long ago when her brother essentially asked Maya that same question. At the time, she couldn't give Rafe an answer, yet now she had to figure it out. She had to make the choice.

It was a back-and-forth game with some good goals interspersed with occasionally sloppy play. Colton redeemed himself for the previous game, with a goal and an assist as San Antonio pulled out a three to two victory. As the opening seconds ticked down, Maya picked up her phone and dialed Frank.

"I don't need until tomorrow morning," she said when he answered. "I've made up my mind."

MICHELE SHRIVER

CHAPTER SIXTEEN

Maya's phone buzzed, signaling another text message. She knew who it was from before she even glanced at the screen. The Generals game had barely ended the night before when she got the first text from Colton, and plenty more had come in since. If she'd had any concern that she might have shot herself in the foot by effectively choosing Colton over keeping the NHL beat, only to find out he didn't really want her, the frequent texts helped ease that concern.

She'd told Frank she wouldn't do it. She wouldn't throw Colton under the bus. Brad could have the NHL beat and Maya would cover the high schools. As soon as she'd gotten off the phone with her boss, though, the doubt began to creep in. What if Colton didn't want any more to do with her? Now that the chase was over, and he got her into bed, would he still be interested? Or was it all about the next conquest? Maya didn't want to think she'd given up her dream job for a playboy who could never settle down.

Maya glanced at her phone display.

How are u?

She grimaced a little at the text abbreviation he'd used. Maybe it was the journalist in her, but Maya always liked proper grammar, even in texts. She made a mental note to talk to him about that as she typed her reply.

Fine. Busy working.

So u do still have a job?

Maya contemplated her reply. She hadn't told Colton anything yet about Frank's ultimatum, her decision, or her new position, figuring it was something better discussed in person. She had to tell him something, though. He'd asked repeatedly what was going on.

Yes. I'll explain when I see you. When do you get back? Maya chuckled as she sent it, wondering if he would notice that she didn't abbreviate words or use text slang.

Colton's reply came right away. *Early afternoon. Can I see u?*

Maya smiled as she read it. He wanted to see her, and she couldn't wait to see him.

How about lunch at Paloma Blanca? I'll meet you there. She wondered if he would recognize the significance of the restaurant choice.

Sounds great. A real date this time. ;) See u there.

Maya typed a quick reply wishing Colton a safe flight, then set her phone down and returned her attention her computer screen. Poring over statistics of high school football games was nowhere near as enjoyable as watching the Generals games from the press box, but Maya vowed to find the good in her position and make it as rewarding as possible. Today, she was writing about a local high school football star who was being recruited by both Baylor and The University of Texas. There was a good deal about anxiety about where he would sign. No, it wasn't professional sports, but it was still big news for the city. People cared. And they'd be counting on Maya to deliver the information. She was still a reporter, and a damn good one. And in a few hours, she had a date with one of the best players in the NHL, who also happened to be sexy as sin. She'd be just fine.

Maya worked without a break for the rest of the morning, until it was time to leave for lunch. She was almost out the door when Frank called to her.

"Hey, Dominguez?"

"Yes?"

Frank hesitated for a second. "You understand, right? That I'm just doing what I have to do?"

Maya nodded. It was a business, and a tough one. She'd known that going in. "And you understand that I'm just doing what *I* have to do?" She didn't know for sure where this thing with Colton would ultimately lead, but she knew she had to find out.

"I get it, yeah," Frank said. "I just hope this guy's worth it."

Maya smiled. "I think he is." Maybe it was a gamble, but wasn't everything in life?

***

The team plane had barely landed in San Antonio and Colton was on his way to meet Maya. Thankfully, Coach gave the players the rest of the day off. They'd reconvene the next morning to get ready for the home opener.

Colton walked into the restaurant and noticed Maya already seated at a table. The same table they'd dined at together back on the first day of training camp. It now seemed like ages ago.

Maya stood to greet him as Colton approached the table, and he gave her a kiss on the cheek. "Thank you for meeting me." He'd been afraid she might not want to.

"Thank you for asking me." She sat back down, and he took the seat opposite her. "How was your flight?"

"Not bad. Everyone's in a pretty good mood after last night." The atmosphere had certainly been better than on the flight from Montreal.

"I'm sure." Maya smiled. "You played a great game."

"So you watched it?" Colton perked up knowing that.

Maya nodded. "I went to a sports bar. They were showing it on all the screens. Quite a crowd too. You guys definitely have some fans."

"And do they all hate me?" Colton asked. "You know, after Montreal..."

"No." Maya shook her head. "Oh, there were some doubters at the beginning last night, but you silenced them pretty quickly." She chuckled. "After two minutes and forty-three seconds, to be exact."

She knew the time of the goal, down to the second. Colton wasn't surprised. "You're something else, you know that?"

"Hey, I may be off the hockey beat, but I'm still a sports reporter."

"And a good one," Colton said. "So what happened, exactly? I expected to see you in Ottawa, and that Smith guy was there. And you haven't said anything in your texts." He hated to think she was off the beat for good, that he might have cost Maya her job. "I'm guessing it's about the article in Sports Chatter." The only other possibility was Maya not wanting anything to do with him, but since she was there, that didn't seem to be the case.

"Yes. My boss saw it. He...was not very pleased."

Colton sucked in a breath. He hated that she was in trouble, and all because of him. "So they pulled you off the beat."

Maya took a drink of water, then set the glass down. "Yes and no."

Colton frowned. "What does that mean? Are you on the beat or not?"

"Not," Maya said. "But Frank gave me a choice." Her lips curled in a wry smile. "If you call it that."

From the tone of her voice, it was clear Maya didn't. "Sounds more like he gave you an ultimatum."

Maya laughed mirthlessly. "It's all in the interpretation." She picked up the water glass again. "I could keep the beat, never see you again outside the job, and spin a story that the Chatter article was correct. You only used me for favorable press, and being a stupid, gullible woman, I fell for it. I look bad, but you look worse, so the paper comes out ahead, at least a little." She took a drink. "Or I could give up the beat, keep you, and be reassigned to high school sports."

"High school?" Colton exhaled sharply. "Isn't that a little harsh?" He'd never met Maya's boss, but already didn't like him.

"Hey, it's Texas. High school football is king here." Maya managed a smile. "I'm already enjoying it."

"So you're saying you..." Colton's voice trailed off.

"I told Frank to shove it, and chose the chance at a future with you." She chewed on her bottom lip in that adorable way of hers. "I'm not going to regret that am I?"

"I can't promise you that," Colton said, and immediately regretted the words. He was bad at this. He'd have to get better. "What I mean is I'm not a fortune teller. I'm just a hockey player and a guy who loves you and who plans on doing something every day to show you how much." He reached across the table and took her hand. "Is that enough for you?"

"It's enough." There was no hesitation in her voice and no fear in her loves. Only love.

EPILOGUE

Colton pulled the car to a stop in the players' parking lot at the arena and turned to Maya. "I like you in that jersey. A lot."

Maya glanced down at maroon and silver jersey she wore, sporting the Generals logo on the front and Colton's name and the number nine on the back. No doubt about it, she was officially a fan now. Two months had passed since she'd declined Frank's 'offer' to keep her job as a beat reporter in exchange for giving up her relationship with Colton, and never once had she regretted it.

Covering high school sports was a step down, yes, but Maya found enjoyment in the job. She'd also introduced Colton to the venerable institution known as high school football in Texas. Sometimes, he even accompanied her to a game and instead of sitting in the press box, they sat in the bleachers with the rest of the fans, just two people on a date.

She now sat in the stands at Generals games, usually in a section a few rows behind the San Antonio bench with the other girlfriends and wives of the players. Each time, Maya wore Colton's jersey with pride. This game, though, was a little bit different. Before taking her usual seat in the arena, Maya would be joining other wives and girlfriends—WAGs, they were called—for the Generals Charity Foundation holiday Toys for Tots drive.

"I like wearing the jersey," she said. "I'm just a little nervous about tonight."

"Don't be." Colton squeezed her hand. "It's collecting toys for needy kids. Nothing to be nervous about."

"Not that. I'm fine with that," Maya said. "You know..." It was the first official WAG event of the season, and thus Maya's official coming out party as Colton Tremblay's significant other. Maybe it was silly, but she was nervous about what people would think.

"What I know is that once people get a look at you, they'll think I'm the luckiest guy in the world," Colton said. "Which is exactly how I feel."

"And you make me feel like the luckiest woman in the world," Maya said. "I just don't want people wondering what you're doing with me when you can have any woman in the world."

Colton chuckled. "That's overly generous estimation of my success with women, for sure. Not that it matters. The only one I want is you."

Once, Maya would have questioned the sincerity of that statement. Now she knew Colton spoke the truth. He'd made good on his promise to show her every day that he loved her. Tonight, after the game, he'd promised to join her family for a midnight celebration in honor of the Virgin of the Guadalupe. He could have begged off, claiming exhaustion from the game, and Maya would have understood. Instead, Colton embraced the opportunity to get to know her family better.

"I have to get inside," Colton said. "I'll see you after the game. And I love you." He leaned over the console and gave her a kiss.

"I love you too."

They got out of the car and Maya watched Colton go the players' entrance before she went to meet the other WAGs to prepare for the toy drive. There was still an hour and a half before the arena would open to the public, but there was a lot to be done.

"Hey, Maya." A blond woman sporting Seth Rollins' jersey greeted her.

Maya smiled. Her first impression of Rollins wasn't a favorable one, but she'd gotten past it. At any rate, she liked his fiancée. "Hi Angie."

"Sold out crowd tonight," Angie said. "The drive should be a success."

"That's great," another woman said. "I'm so excited about this. I told my dad I had to be a part of it, no matter what."

Maya studied the face of Meryl Johnson, the youngest daughter of the Generals owner. She might be young, spoiled and a little naive in the ways of the world, but it was hard not to like her enthusiasm. "We're glad you're here, Meryl." Maya noticed Meryl also wore a Generals team jersey, hers with Nik Brantov's number forty-four on the back. "And what's up with the jersey? Is there something you're not telling us?"

"Oh, this?" Meryl's cheeks reddened. "Maybe a little wishful thinking on my part."

###

Books by Michele Shriver

Women's Fiction:

After Ten
Tears and Laughter
Aggravated Circumstances

Contemporary Romance:

Finding Forever
Leap of Faith
The Art of Love
Starting Over
Love & Light (coming spring 2015)

The Men of the Ice Novellas:

Playing for Keeps
Crossing the Line (Fall 2015)
Winning it All (2016)

Boxed Sets:

Heroes to Swoon For
Spring Into Love (May 2015)
Score One For Love (August 2015)

Thank you for reading. I hope you enjoyed the story and will consider posting an honest review of this book on the site you purchased it from.

Keep reading for a special preview of Crossing the Line, next in the Men of the Ice series.

MICHELE SHRIVER

Crossing the Line

Chapter One

Nikolai Brantov knotted his tie and ran his fingers through his damp hair, trying to spike the top exactly the way he liked it. When he first moved to the United States from his native Russia five months before to realize his dream of playing in the National Hockey League, he not only had to learn a new language—one he still struggled with—he had to learn new customs and traditions too. Among those were the expectations of being a player in the NHL, including the team dress code which left Nik primping more in front of a mirror as he prepared to leave the arena after a game than he might to get ready for a date. Not that he had any time for dating. Practice, games and English lessons filled most of his days, and that suited Nik fine. He'd left his family and his homeland at the age of nineteen to move to North America to play hockey, not meet women.

"Great game tonight, Nik," the team captain, Colton Tremblay, said as he came up beside Nik.

Nik nodded at Colton. "Thanks. You too." The San Antonio Generals beat the Winnipeg Jets three to two in overtime, and Nik scored the winning goal. His first season in the NHL, and the expansion Generals' first season in the league, were both going well. The country might be unfamiliar, and the rink sizes a little different, but hockey was still hockey, and on the ice was where Nik felt at home.

"You're going to stop by the foundation table and see how the toy drive went, right?" Colton asked.

"Yes. I will." Nik would because he knew it was

expected of him. It was almost Christmas, and the Generals charity foundation held a drive to collect toys for needy children. Many of his teammates, included Colton, were excited about the event because their girlfriends and wives had organized it. Being single, it was less of a big deal to Nik. Still, as much as he would feel completely out of place, it was an important team event and Nik had to make an appearance.

"I'll head over there with you," Colton said. "I'm anxious to see my girl."

Nik nodded at him and they left the locker room together. Of course Colton was anxious to get there to see his girlfriend again. With no one there waiting for Nik to greet him with a kiss and congratulate him on a good game, he planned to make a quick appearance—the minimum expected of him—and head home. Such that it was. 'Home' to Nik right now meant staying with a host family in San Antonio while he acclimated to his new city and new country.

Sure enough, as they approached the Generals Foundation charity booth, Colton's girlfriend came over gave him a kiss on the cheek. "Nice game, as usual," she said, then nodded in Nik's direction. "You too."

"Thanks."

"The toy drive was a huge success," Maya continued. "Come see everything we collected." She led the way to the boxes of children's toys, dressed in a maroon and silver Generals jersey with Colton's name and number on the back. Surrounding the table was a group of other women, similarly dressed to support their player.

"Hey Nik, is there something you're not telling us?" Colton asked, as his eyes darted to a young woman in the group.

Nik recognized her as Meryl Johnson, the daughter of the Generals team owner. They'd never met before, although Nik had seen her at a couple of team events. His impression of her was that she was spoiled and liked to get her way, but maybe that was to be expected from the daughter of a billionaire. And maybe it wasn't fair to judge someone he'd never so much as exchanged a word with. She was attractive, that was for sure, with her long brown hair pulled back in a ponytail. She, too, wore a Generals jersey, and it took Nik a moment to realize what Colton referred to. The jersey Meryl wore was Nik's.

Before he could answer Colton that he had no idea what that was about, Meryl approached him. "Hi there. I don't think we've been formally introduced," she said, extending a hand. "I'm Meryl Johnson."

"Yes. Mr. Johnson's daughter." Nik shook her hand. "Nikolai Brantov."

***

He said it as if he thought she might not know his name, and Meryl appreciated his unassuming nature. So many of the athletes she'd encountered had big egos, and Nikolai had every reason to as well. The hockey season might be only a few months old, but the young Russian had already made an impression on the league. Meryl's father remarked every day that Nik was a superstar in the making.

Meryl smiled at him. "I know who you are." After all, her father owned the team, and Meryl made it her business to know about the players he employed. And why shouldn't she? Hockey players were hot, and in Meryl's estimation, none more so than Nikolai Brantov, with his gray eyes and spiked brown hair that Meryl longed to run her fingers through.

She'd first noticed him during the summer's NHL draft, when he became the first-ever draft choice of the San Antonio Generals. He appeared awkward in his first interviews, and a little overwhelmed, immediately intriguing Meryl. Was that his true personality, or a byproduct of the circumstances he found himself in? It couldn't be easy moving to a new country and having to learn a new language at the age of nineteen.

From that moment, Meryl wanted to learn as much about him as possible, so she sought out all the information she could. She knew Nik hailed from the Russian city of Maykop, that his favorite color was orange, and he liked to eat steak and baked potatoes. He listed the Pittsburgh Penguins as his favorite NHL team and his countryman, Evgeni Malkin, as his favorite player. And even knowing all of that, Nik remained an enigma to Meryl.

"I'm wearing your jersey, after all," she said, and did a little twirl so he could see his name and number on the back. Her choice of attire had raised a few eyebrows among the wives and girlfriends' who'd put together the event, and who proudly sported their man's jerseys, but Meryl didn't care. Her father owned the team, she could wear whatever she wanted.

"Yes," Nik said, nodding. "It's...what's the word?" He frowned a little. "Bold of you?"

He was so cute in his uncertainty. Meryl knew he had a tutor working with him on his English, a job she would have gladly volunteered for. In fact, she had, only half-jokingly. It was, after all, her college major. Not surprisingly, Daddy had vetoed that idea and warned her that Nik, and everyone else on the team, was off-limits to Meryl. "That's me. Bold," Meryl said.

"It looks nice on you," Nik said, causing Meryl's

heart to flutter a little.

"Better on you, I think. Especially when you scored the winning goal."

Nik shrugged. "I was in the right place and got a good pass from Colton."

Definitely unassuming, Meryl decided. And hot. She kept going back to that one. Damn her father and his prohibitions. He never wanted her to have any fun. "What are you doing tonight?" she asked. "I just have to help put this stuff away," she gestured to the boxes of toys they'd collected during the charity drive, "then my dad is having a little party up in his box, if you want to join me." He'd already called her bold. Meryl figured she might as well live up to it.

Nik hesitated before answering, giving Meryl hope that perhaps he'd seriously consider the invitation, but the hope was dashed when he shook his head. "No, thank you. I need to go home."

Meryl knew 'home' to Nik was a family of strangers hosting him in their house, and she questioned his need—or desire—to rush back to that, but she didn't press the issue. "Have a good night, then. It was nice to meet you."

"You as well, Miss Johnson," he said.

She watched him walk away, admiring how his suit fit his body. Okay, he hadn't accepted her invitation. Meryl hadn't really expected him to. At least they'd shared a few words, finally. The rest would happen in due time. Meryl was accustomed to getting everything she wanted, and she'd already decided she wanted Nik Brantov.

Author's Note and Acknowledgements

The idea for a new book can come from virtually anywhere, I've found, but I didn't have to look very far for the idea for this one. I love hockey and hockey players, so it's not much of a stretch that I would decide to write a series about hockey players. I had a good time writing Colton and Maya's story. I hoped you enjoyed reading it and will also look forward to future Men of the Ice Novellas, featuring Nik and Meryl (Crossing the Line) and Trev and Dani (Winning it All). Who knows- there might even be more books to come about the San Antonio Generals Men of the Ice and the women who love them.

As always, I am grateful to everyone who has helped me along the way in my publishing journey. Your support and encouragement means the world.

I must also thank my beta readers for all of their helpful feedback in making this story shine. I may not have taken all of your advice, but please know I appreciate all of your efforts and that you helped improve the story in immeasurable ways.

Cover design by Sprinkles on Top Studios.

Michele Shriver writes women's fiction and contemporary romance. Her books feature flawed-but-likeable characters in real-life settings. She's not afraid to break the rules, but never stops believing in happily ever after. Michele counts among her favorite things a good glass of wine, a hockey game, and a sweet and sexy book boyfriend, not necessarily in that order.

Contact:
www.micheleshriver.com
twitter.com/micheleshriver
Facebook page: Author Michele Shriver
micheleshriver@gmail.com

For contests, special gifts, advance reader copies of my books and the chance to hang out and chat and keep up to date on all my publishing news, please consider joining my Facebook group:

https://www.facebook.com/groups/721292531291721/

PLAYING FOR KEEPS